INTERRUPTION:
The Gospel According to Crystal Justine

Tracey Michae'l Lewis

INTERRUPTION:
The Gospel According to Crystal Justine

Tracey Michae'l Lewis

NewSEASON BOOKS
Philadelphia, PA

ISBN: 978-0-9718920-7-1

Published in the United States by:
NewSEASON Books
P.O. Box 52545
Philadelphia, PA 19115
newseasonbooks@gmail.com

Editing:
Cynthia Graham
C.T. Editorial Services, Intl. ~ cteditorial@yahoo.com

Cover Design:
Andy Musser

I'm grateful for the journey and those who were/are my support along the way. - TMLG

"So, go now and write all this down.
Put it in a book
So that the record will be there
to instruct the coming generations"
- Isaiah 30:8 (The Message)

Prologue

Natas was the second lieutenant archai of this specific battalion of demons – Chicago Principality, Southern Region. He'd risen through the ranks and was probably one of only a few of the originals that were assigned to this family of women. In fact, he'd come on board in the early 1800s when CJ's great-great-great-grandmother was born in what is now known as Texas. She carried in her **the great destiny** and the General, Natas' demanding and determined leader, was determined to thwart its manifestation at all costs. So far, they've been relatively successful. In fact, the assignment seemed pretty simple. At the most, rob them of their un-surrendered souls. At the very least, stop the line of women in CJ's family from realizing the power that lies inside of them and, as a result, eliminate the Enemy's ability to use them for any good in the world.

Natas proudly takes the credit for Sasha. Yes, there was nothing they could do about losing her soul. That was pretty much a done deal when she uttered those horrible words and her spirit slipped from the grasp of darkness. However, he gladly descended to a new low in his career when he was able to take her life before she ever realized **the great destiny**. Yet, in spite of their best efforts, they could not prevent her from giving birth to another girl child. Another child born with that special gift. Another chance at redemption.

CJ has proven to be a much more challenging target. It appears that she has some kind of hedge around her, so Natas, known to be an excellent strategist, decides to modify his approach. If he can break down the people around her, the ones who have supported the child and protected her with their prayers, then maybe, just maybe, he can get to her, even kill her like he did her mother. Time, however, is of the essence.

Part One:
Introductions

Chapter 1

I assure you, I'm nothing like my mother.

Some people may think that's a harsh thing to say, especially if I'm implying that there is something wrong with being like my mother. I'm sure they are probably right. The problem is that they don't have my life. They don't understand what it's like to live in the shadow of a mother that you've never known. It's hard to appreciate something or someone who's never been an active part of your life. A mother that, from what I'm told, was beautiful and captivating and charming and any of the other terms of endearment people use to describe Ms. Sasha Renee. All of the things I am not. No, people say I'm cute, *if* I could lose about 10lbs. I'll even get intelligent, *if* I was just smart enough to get a real job and keep a man. Well, frankly, if being just cute and intelligent keeps me from being dead, then I'll take it. Because, despite all of those wonderful attributes, isn't that how my mother ended up? Dead? I'm not going to sugarcoat how I feel about that for the sake of decorum.

I'll admit there's a part of me that desperately wishes I felt another way. I do find myself wishing that "mommy" was synonymous with love and nurturing instead of ambivalence and abandonment. Unfortunately, that warm and fuzziness is trumped by my lack of a point of reference. I realize this might sound like an excuse for not trying, and maybe it is, but excuse or not, it's my reality. A reality that I'm determined to turn into one very long "lemons to lemonade" moment.

If only I could get over some things.

You see, I am, at the very least, uncomfortable with myself. In my greatest state of self-uncertainty, I'm an imposter floating between a fear of failure and a fear of my success. I want things in my life that seem so unattainable that I am, in essence, swimming against a fierce current that prevents me from reaching my destination. The only thing left for me is faith. The little bit of it that I've been able to muster. Faith that where I end, Christ begins. I can thank my father for that. Langston Germaine. An awesome man whose faith has shown me that where the footsteps of my tumultuous life may end, God's provision can begin, carrying me to the finish line located in the center of His will.

Nonetheless, I still have several issues to deal with immediately. Fear. Insecurity. Control. All stemming from the idea that I'm not good enough. You shouldn't be surprised I know this about myself. Most people need a self-help or a pseudo-psychologist/talk show host to tell them what they already know. I just decided to skip the middle man. These challenges, as I like to call them, have been constants in all aspects of my life. Even in my relationships, where it would seem I would be the most comfortable, I tend to linger on the idea that I have to do "extra" things to garner the love and attention of people, even the men I may occasionally date. In fact, I come across beautiful men all the time and the reality is, I always end up believing they wouldn't be attracted to me because of my big smile, unruly hair, the tendency of my weight to fluctuate, or any other superficial reason my mind can conjure.

Sheltered. That's the only word I can think of when describing the life I've lived thus far. It's like when my mother died, my father placed all of his energy into his work, eventually becoming Dean of the Business School at DePaul University and, of course, in raising me. Protecting me. At least as much as he could. He never remarried and I'm not sure how I feel about that. On the one hand, I loved it being just me and my dad against the world. But as I grew up, I began to wonder about the sadness I saw in his eyes. I'm observant that way. There was this silent longing that would shadow his eyes as though he wished he had someone to share his life with him. When I'd ask him about it, he'd brush me off by saying my mother was the one he'd loved, that no one compared to her, and it wouldn't be fair to make any woman try. You see what I mean? My mother's legacy has even been a hindrance to my dad. Neither of us can get away from Sasha if we tried. But I plan to. Just you wait and see.

Anyway, when it comes to any conversation I have with my dad about my mother, I always seem to say the wrong thing. I don't think it's intentional because I would never want to hurt my father in that way. On the other hand, I've had to live with his fragility my entire life and at times, I find myself testing him. The other day at lunch was no exception.

We'd decided to meet at Dahlia's, this hot, new, eclectic restaurant on State Street. Periodically, dad and I will meet for lunch to update each other on what's going on in our lives, just the way we used to when I was a little girl. Only now, we exchange pleasantries over sushi and white wine instead of peanut butter and jelly and milk. When dad walked into the room, I couldn't help but notice how the women in the restaurant responded to him. At nearly sixty, Langston Germaine was an attractive man, as far as dads go. His salt-and-pepper hair was neatly cut into a short fade, and for a man his age, he was in great shape. In spite of living with a heartache that never went away, there was something just beneath the surface of him that seemed to speak to young girls and grandmas alike. It had always been like that. Little did they know that, like dad's heart, his dating life had been shut down for a very long time, with no sign of a grand re-opening.

Since I could see him before he could see me, I raised my hand so he could find me in the sea of lunchtime lingerers attempting to be as sophisticated and chic as the place they were dining, but managing to only blend in to its predictably retro decor. Oblivious to the estrogen-driven stares, he made his way across the room in his trademark, long strides as our eyes met.

"Hey, sweetheart," he said.

"Hey, Daddy!"

"Been waiting long?"

"Yes, hours."

Dad smiled at my exaggeration.

"Oh, zip it, silly!"

I laughed.

"So, you have me at one of these shmancy, fancy places for lunch, huh?"

"Well, I've gotta get you to spend some money on your only daughter some way!"

"I think I heard something similar to that the last time I was here."

I didn't understand what he meant by that, but I soon found out.

"What! I didn't know that you'd eaten here before. You should have told me!"

"Well, not exactly before."

He paused and stared at me as though he was playing the staring game with a ghost. I suspect he was.

"I brought your mother here 30 years ago, only then it was the Weber Grill."

Snapping out of his trance, he continued. "You look so much like her."

Oh, oh. I tried so hard to keep my emotional composure, but I felt it coming. It was like the all-too familiar look of worn nostalgia mixed with a withering hopelessness that sent the words flying out of my mouth.

"Not only do I doubt that I do, I really wish that she'd stop interrupting our lunches."

A contortionist could not have twisted his or her face in more directions than my father did right then. He winced as if he had been stabbed and, once again, my mouth had been the assailant. I tried to clean it up.

"I'm sorry, daddy. That was…"

"…uncalled for?" He finished.

14

"Insensitive? Stupid? Wrong?" He continued.

"Yes, dad, I'm all of those things."

A heavy sigh escaped dad's lips as he considered the implications of my sudden emotional martyrdom.

"No, you're not. The *words* were, yes, but you're not those things, Sasha…"

He tried to hit rewind just as quickly as I had a moment   earlier.

"…I mean, CJ."

It wasn't the first time that had happened.

"Daddy, please don't take this the wrong way. But it's been 25 years since Sasha…" I noticed his posture became rigid at my addressing her by her first name, so I quickly corrected myself.

"…my mother died. I know how much you loved her, but don't you think she'd want you to move on?"

He smiled.

"Knowing her, she probably would."

"So?"

"So, it's just not that easy, CJ."

"Nothing worth doing is easy. Isn't that what you taught me?"

He smiled again.

"Using my words against your old man, huh?"

I knew he was trying to change the subject and I let him. There was already too much said for one day.

"Better your words than mine, right?"

We both broke out into a loud, nervous, overcompensating laughter. Case closed for now.

***

I get asked all the time what it was like to be raised by just my father. What happened when I had "girl" stuff to discuss? Well, fortunately, my dad was really good about things. Growing up, I could talk to him about everything. Well, *almost* everything. I definitely have my secrets. Things that I know would break his heart if he knew about them. Some of which would probably rip my entire family apart.

But, I'm not ready to talk about those things and I don't know if I'll ever be.

There are women in my life though. Almost too many, if you ask me. My Aunt Kara and Aunt Toni are like my big sisters. They were friends of my mom who kind of adopted me as their daughter as soon as I was born. Aunt Kara is married to my father's best friend, Benson. That's an interesting story all by itself. Then, there's my godmother, Ms. Cassie and Nana, my grandmother. All of these women have played a major part in my life — giving me advice and sharing their various wisdoms. I think in a way they think they can prevent me from making the same mistakes my mother made as a young woman.

As a matter of fact, it was two of these women who sat me down when I turned eighteen and with the tearful eyes of a tragic memory relived, told me how my mother died. Up until then, I was just told she died in childbirth.

***

I remember it being a frigid day in November. The kind where simply stepping outside was all the reason the Chicago wind needed to slice your face off. I'd finally decided to attend one of my Aunt Toni's and Aunt Kara's monthly spa days. I usually passed on the event because it was another remnant of days long gone when my mother and her friends would meet for a little "pampering and peacemaking," as they called it. This month, however, I was stressed out and, if I'm honest, looked a mess. I'd spent the last four weeks finishing six essays for five different college and scholarship applications. I reasoned that a spa day couldn't be all that bad if they'd kept up the tradition for all these years. I mean, I could endure the spirit of Sasha for a few hours in exchange for a massage and pedicure, right?

"Whaaaat! Look who the cat done drug in," screamed Aunt Toni when I walked through the parlor doors. At 5'9 with a short, gray-haired Ceasar cut and a fierce, red Dolce & Gabbana pants suit, Toni looked every bit of the mature, sophisticated ex-model that she was. In fact, I don't think I'd ever seen her un-fabulous.

"Hush, Toni! Hey, baby girl. Glad you finally decided to join the old ladies."

This was my Aunt Kara. She was also beautiful, just in a less-obvious kind of way. With a bright, birch complexion, trademark freckles and the same wild, golden curly hair she'd had for all of my life. She made being a "plain Jane" seem like a compliment. She'd gained a few pounds over the years, though. Probably due to a marriage that overflowed with drama with every passing month. Nevertheless, her natural beauty and sweet demeanor always made me think of what I would have wanted in a mother if I had one.

"Aunt Toni, why you always messing with me?" I said with mock sarcasm.

"Because you're too cute for words and I just can't stand it." She said this as she leaned over in her pedicure chair and kissed me on my cheek. I smiled. She always knew how to flip it and make me feel good.

Surprisingly, the spa day started off pretty cool. No reminiscing and no explanations. For a moment, I felt like just one of the girls and the warmth that often lay dormant in my heart began to seep below the surface, making a b-line for my soul. Today, I thought to myself, I was going to be able to keep my attitude, which I bring wherever I go in case things get too difficult for me to handle, in my purse and out of sight.

Let me explain something. I'm quite aware of my resistance to accepting anything that might offer me peace regarding the big Sasha-sized hole I have in my heart. Even when I'm sincerely trying to be positive and open about it, there's this tug in my gut that keeps me from going all the way there. I've learned to live with it most of the time. In fact, I'm really not as bitter as I might seem. I do have those days where I find myself doing my own reminiscing. The best way I can. I will settle in my big chair and flip through the millions of photo albums my dad has kept over the years. I even find myself smiling back at that gorgeous woman in the pictures. The one with the big smile looking back at me with what seems like the same curiosity I have about her. In my day to day life, there are certain things I do and say that seem foreign to me until I realize it's her essence and the essence of my Nana coming out in ways I could have never known or experienced. And yes, if only in my quiet times, I admit to embracing it.

But—and this is a big but—it's situations like the one that cold day at the spa, where I feel crowded by other people's affection for my mother, so much so that my natural reaction is to deflect or lash out. I knew that as soon as I felt the familiar feeling of the bottom dropping out of my stomach at the sound of her name, I should have made a quick exit out of the spa. But I didn't.

"Don't forget to pick your color," Toni said as I returned from the massage room and prepared for my pedicure.

I stood in front of the wall mount that held hundreds of bottles of nail polish for about ten minutes before settling on a color I thought suited me.

"What did you get?" Kara asked.

"Talk of the Town Brown," I said, thinking nothing of it. It was Fall and the turning leaves inspired me to choose this deep, golden-brown hue.

"Wow." Kara placed her hand over her mouth, looking over at Toni in a way that suggested a mixture of surprise and sadness.

"Wow is right," Toni said.

"What? What's wrong? Y'all don't think this color goes well with my complexion?"

Toni, whose back was facing me because she was seated along the wall at a nail dryer, turned around.

"No, it's not that. The color is beautiful."

Then I heard Kara say it. At least I think I heard her say it. The words came from the direction in which she was sitting, but the sound of them was more like an echo inside of my head.

"That was your mother's favorite color."

Toni caught me rolling my eyes and I think I intended for her to see it.

"What's your deal, C.J? Every time your mother's name is mentioned, you act as though someone is slapping you across the face."

"Do I?"

Kara chimed in. "Yes, you do."

"Well, maybe I'm just tired of hearing about what Sasha did and what Sasha said, and what Sasha wore. I'm eighteen and I'm officially tired of hearing about it."

"Don't you want to know what your mother was like," Kara asked in her soft but imploring voice.

I didn't know how to answer that. In a way, I did. I wanted to know that more than anything else. In another way, I felt burdened by it. Like I could never live up to her and I would never be able to stop trying.

"Sometimes. But she seems so perfect and I don't know, sometimes it's hard to hear how loved she was without thinking that I could never be loved like that."

"Perfect?" Toni stood up from the nail dryer and walked over to me. She was looking down, blowing on her fingers and talking at the same time.

"Girl, puh-lease! Sasha was far from perfect. As a matter of fact, she was off the hook sometimes. But we knew her heart and so to have her taken away from us..."

Kara tried to get Toni's attention before she could say anymore. Too late.

"What do you mean *taken* away from you?"

I remember feeling this rush of emotion. My heart was beating so fast I thought it would break the skin and leap out of my chest.

Toni looked at Kara who shook her head.

"Langston never told her. He wanted to wait until she was older."

I kept looking back and forth between the two women who served as surrogate mothers for me. They, in turn, held a silent conversation with their eyes and after a few moments, settled on a decision. They decided to tell me the truth about my mother's death.

Chapter 2

Seven years later and I don't think I've processed it completely. I honestly don't know what I should feel. I mean, I'm human. I feel compassion for people who have terrible things happen to them. But I'm pretty sure I'm not supposed to have the same feelings for my mother's death as I do for the random murder that is reported on the nightly news. But, I didn't know her. I don't know, maybe my reaction is rooted in the fact that I wish I did. Maybe then I'd know more about myself.

This much I do know. My name is Crystal Justine Germaine. As I'm sure you've figured out by now, my family and friends call me CJ for short. I was named after Madame C.J. Walker, the first black businesswoman to become a millionaire with her line of beauty products. I guess that's not so bad. Not that I make anywhere near a million dollars, but if it's true your child's name stays with them forever, then I don't think that mine is so bad. It adds some meaning to my life.

My dad says that by twenty-five years old, most people are seeking some kind of purpose in life, and I guess I'm no exception. Although, I must say I'm ahead of many other folks my age, in that I do have some idea of what I was born to do. I wasn't kidding when I spoke about being *extra* observant as a child. I am. In fact, it's that eye for detail, that ability to see past the surface, which has contributed to my rising success as a writer. It seems like I've been writing stories my entire life. Ever since I was eight years old and my dad bought me the prettiest journal covered with little brown girls in pink ballerina dresses, I've been capturing the various memories and moments of life with my pen. From the young girls in patent leather shoes and petticoats taking their group Sunday school picture on Easter, to the equally impatient pigeons fighting for the last pieces of bread on a quiet Chicago street, you name it, I've written about it.

I find I'm able to discern God's amazing glory that exists among the rather ordinary nouns *(people, places and things)* I see on a daily basis. From childhood until now, I've written for journals, newspapers, magazines and have at least five anthologies under my belt. I'm now working, or I should say struggling, through my first novel. The ironic thing is, the ability to see past the surface seems to escape me once I put my laptop down and attempt to have a real life. Maybe that's why I keep writing. I'm always writing. Because when I'm writing, I can tell stories that only require me to dig into my characters' souls, instead of searching my own. Another writer once tried convincing me that the two were connected and that if I ever wanted to be truly significant as a writer, I was going to have to surrender some part of myself for the story's sake. That scares me.

Jonathan would agree that it's fear. He thinks I have a fear of letting anyone get too close to me and my heart. That would include fictional characters. He would know, I guess. Jonathan is my best friend. Maybe even my only friend. He's definitely the only one who'd have the nerve to read me in such a way. I met him when I was six years old and my dad moved us to the south side of Chicago so we could be closer to my Nana. Nana had fallen into a deep depression after my mom died and dad thought having me around would lift her spirits. So, we moved into a quiet neighborhood just south of Hyde Park, a middle-class area near the University of Chicago. Though it was a longer commute to DePaul for dad, I think he also needed to be closer to all the things and people that were familiar to him. In the townhouse next door was a sweet, single mother with an adorable, seven-year-old boy. That boy was Jonathan and meeting him changed my life in so many ways.

Can I be truthful for a moment? When I first laid my six-year-old eyes on that little boy, I thought he was the most incredible person I'd ever met. This was even after he punched me in my arm when our parents introduced us to each other for the first time. I cried because it hurt, but it didn't stop me from being his friend. It's possible the assault only made him even more awesome to me because somehow I knew in the language of "boy," that was his way of telling me I was pretty great, too. From that day on, we were joined at the hip.

Up until we were about twelve years old, Jonathan and I were what I like to call the *super*-saved kids on our street. That meant we went to church every Sunday morning, Youth Bible Study on Wednesday nights, and were active members of our youth choir, junior usher board and Bible Drill Team. Jonathan was even a junior deacon. Although church was all we knew, this wasn't a false reality for us, as some of my more agnostic friends would like to believe. Our love for God and our church was an authentic one, rooted in the teachings of our parents and the fact that we weren't yet heavily influenced by anyone outside of our little world at the time. That, of course, only lasted until Jonathan discovered girls. *Real* girls, he once told me. Not like me. Somehow, I wasn't quite a girl to him, even if I wasn't exactly a boy. And me? Well, I figured out that being a church girl came with some very unwanted perceptions of me. At twelve, I realized that, besides my family, the people in my life fell into two categories. There were those who thought me to be a "goody two shoes" because I was the revered Professor Germaine's daughter and then there were those that pitied me because I was the late, great Sasha Renee's daughter. In trying to define myself in the middle of a hormone-raging adolescence, I guess I became lost between these two perceptions of me. "Deceptions" is probably a more accurate word to describe that place.

23

It's not that I became some horrible monster in my teens. I still had respect for my father and didn't really want to do anything that would bring him any public embarrassment. However, I was extremely mischievous. Ms. Cassie, my godmother, used to say I was sneaky. The fact of the matter is I knew how to play the game—the role of a good, little Christian girl. Admittedly, I actually *had* experienced the authentic and amazing power of the Spirit as a young child, yet in my naiveté, I began to observe how pretending to be good, while actually *doing* the opposite, could be much more advantageous to me in the short term.

The first time I tried my hand at this duality was when I was eleven years old. Every Sunday, the church held a youth service downstairs in the basement. Children in grades K through 5 were separated into two groups: girls and boys. Upon entering sixth grade, however, the service went co-ed. Everyone, including me, looked forward to that. Not only were we allowed to be with the opposite sex, we also got a chance to hold leadership positions. So, there were junior deacons who collected the penny offerings and, mimicking the cadence of the adults, said all of the prayers. It was actually pretty funny when I think about it now. Imagine skinny, brown boys with fresh haircuts and high booties wearing too-big black suits.

"Faaather God, who is the HEAD of myyy life, thank ya' for the offering. Bless those who had it to give and those who did not. May it be uuuused for the UPkeep of YOUR kingdommm. In the matchless, MAAAHVelous name of Jesus, the Christ, Amen?"

Even as kids, we knew we should respond even though we weren't quite sure why it was posed as a question. "Amen." And for emphasis, the old men in training would repeat, "AAAAAAmennnnnn."

The youth choir gave the A and B selections, and the junior ushers, who were usually high school students, would walk up and down the aisles making sure we were behaving. For me, youth church was even more fun because I could also finally hang with my bmf (best male friend), Jonathan, who was a year older than me and served as a junior deacon.

One Sunday, Jonathan was asked to take the money basket upstairs to the adult service so it could be counted with the general offering. After about thirty minutes, he still hadn't returned, so one of the adults who supervised the youth church asked if anyone would like to go upstairs and find out what happened. Well, of course, at first, no one raised their hand. No one wanted to be the one sent to bring back one of the more popular guys in church, who was most likely playing a little bit of hooky. Then, I had an idea. I raised my hand to volunteer and was sent off to find my friend. As I was leaving the room, I heard the adult in charge say how wonderful it was that I wasn't afraid to take some initiative and be a leader. If only she knew.

As I walked down the hall past one of the Sunday school classrooms, I heard a weird noise. It sounded like someone pretending to be a car or truck. My curiosity got the best of me, so I pushed open the door and found Jonathan trying to impress a few of the high school boys by talking about cars. Jonathan turned around and looked at me with disdain. I put my plan in motion.

"Whatchu want, CJ?"

Before I even answered, I could tell he was embarrassed I was coming to get him at the request of the youth church leader. I didn't want him to feel bad, but I wasn't going to let him talk to me crazy, either. I responded with my hand on my hip and a twist in my neck, typical south-side fashion.

"Whatchu think I want?"

He sighed really loud and walked over to me, stomping the whole way. The high school boys shrugged and kept talking about the Mustang.

"You see I'm busy, girl."

"Yeah, and?"

"So why *you* got to come get me?"

He said it like it would have been okay if anyone else but me came to get him. That hurt my feelings, but didn't stop me.

Jonathan grabbed the now empty offering basket and began walking out of the door and down the hall. I followed behind him and finally caught up to him. As my pulse quickened, I knew it was either now or never.

"Actually, I wanted to show you something."

He stopped walking.

"What?"

He sounded perturbed.

"You don't have to sound so mean."

Jonathan softened a bit. He knew he was more embarrassed than anything and that it wasn't my fault he was going to get in trouble. I also knew that he knew that.

"What did you want to show me?"

"A tarantula."

"A tarantula? Girl, stop playing. Ain't no big ole' spider down here."

"Yes, there is. In the janitor's closet over there." I pointed to the large, gray metal door about five feet away.

"For real?"

I knew that would get him. He may have been trying to impress the older boys with his knowledge of cars, but what twelve-year-old boy isn't intrigued by big bugs?

"Yeah. But I'm scared of it. Do you want to go see it?"

"Uh-huh."

Jonathan walked over to the janitor's closet and slowly opened the door. It was black as night in there, so I closed the gap between us, moving closer to him. He reached out to the wall and turned on the light just as the door slammed behind us.

"So where is it?"

"I think it might have moved under the cabinet."

Jonathan bent down to look under the cabinet shelves.

"I'll turn off the light so it will come out again."

I quickly hit the light switch.

The darkness that enveloped us must have frightened him because he straightened up quickly, just in enough time for me to kiss him. The plan was to kiss him on his lips, but because he jumped up so fast, my lips landed somewhere between his lips and his chin.

"CJ!"

I stood still. I didn't know what to say. Ironically, I prayed. I hoped God wouldn't be so mad that I'd lured my friend into the church's storage room and tried to kiss him that He'd let Jon say something that would break my eleven-year-old heart. I was terrified.

"Ewwwww, what are you doing," Jonathan exclaimed as he feverishly wiped his face of what must have been like the plague, the way he was rubbing. So much for that prayer.

I felt the tears that were building in those few seconds finally reach my eyes as Jonathan's rejection became clear. There was no way I could have understood at that age that Jonathan's reaction was his adolescent uncertainty conflicting with the realization of his mutual feelings. As I ran out of the room and down the hallway back to youth church, my mind was fixed on replaying the incident in the most dramatic of ways. The only thing real to me in that moment was seeing him wipe my teenage love off of his visage. What I didn't see, however, was the smile that crept slowly across Jonathan's face or the warmth that filled his entire body, all of this occurring, of course, after I left.

No, I had no business luring him into the closet in the first place. Yes, after years of personal torment, Jonathan has still been the best friend a person could ever have. But it was that first rejection that would undoubtedly set the stage for the relationships that were to come.

Chapter 3

Mostly because of my naïveté, I've been hurt by love. Too many times to mention. With the exception of my dad, I've never really known what it's like to feel the reciprocal side of love. Whenever I chose to love, the love was never returned. The sad thing is—when I open that door, when I become connected to someone in that way—I can't shut my emotions off. Once my heart opens, it's like those ancient, wooden doors in castles, it takes many men to close it. I want to, though. Close it, I mean. Love makes me feel exposed and naked, which wouldn't necessarily be a bad thing if someone was responding with the same transparency. But they never do.

Sometimes I feel like I'm standing in the garden of Eden, just after being created into this beautiful creature, wonderfully designed as a gift for someone, and that dummy, Adam, hasn't awakened yet.

As a matter of fact, I think I'm going to write about the first family from an entirely different perspective than I've read before, partially because I think it would be cool to do that and partially because I have some serious questions about the whole thing. Like, how much time actually passed between Eve's creation and Adam waking up to see her? If I had to draw any parallels from my own life, I'd say an eternity. And how did Eve know who was her Adam? Yeah, yeah, yeah, I know. God presented her to him. But, get this. If

I, Eve, have never seen Adam before, then I could be mistaking him for the lion, the giraffe, or even a dog frolicking in the grass for all I know. And trust me, I have. Mistaken him for a dog, I mean. Too many times to count.

And why do I find myself frolicking with these counterfeit Adams? Because waiting sucks. I've waited. Patiently, at first. And later, with a bit more urgency. I want to believe that my "Adam" will recognize me. I want to believe that he'll wade through shark-infested waters and leap over mountains to get to me. He has to, doesn't he? He'll recognize that I'm the one that's missing in his life. I'm the bone of his bone and flesh of his flesh...just like the Bible says, right? Unless, of course, he's stupid. Oh, please God, don't let him be stupid. Or, maybe he'll be an egomaniac, waiting for me to come over and shake him out of his slumber. To stroke his ego enough times so he'll feel good about himself, while leaving me worn, stressed and doing work I wasn't meant to do. Uggghhh, I hope not! Or, maybe he'll be scared. Maybe he sees me, but he's hiding out of fear of what I might think about him.

Yeah, I know. Pull it back, CJ. Just a little over the top, right? My imagination gets the best of me sometimes. The fact is, I've always been captivated with the idea of love. Obtaining it and keeping it. Managing it and being damaged by it. I've always tried to decide whether I was truly worthy of love's touch or whether someone else was worthy of me giving my little piece of love up. It seems like I've spent a lifetime on the phone with girlfriends recounting my adventures with this thing. Constantly hiding behind my pen trying to capture small glimpses of it. Praying to God that the love that finds me will come in some splendid form like six feet tall, chocolate skin and beautiful, white teeth.

I like teeth.

But the joke is on me. I think God finds it funny to only send variations of that fantasy. Chocolate but 5' 2". Tall but with jacked-up teeth. Ha! Ha! Ha!

On top of that, I hear that voice in my head whispering nasty nothings about my own eligibility for a mate. Of course, this only seems to only occur when I stare intently at my form in the mirror, wishing away my size 12 frame. I think I'm searching for my inner size 6 and secretly thinking that certain physical enhancements will make me more appealing to men. It's a ploy I use to forget about the healing that I really need on the inside. But like every other woman in the world, I often fall prey to the lies that are told about me nowadays.

I'll admit (since I'm admitting everything else) that my failed grandiose search for external affairs of the heart (translation: finding love in some other human form) are simply manifestations of the things I've internalized over the years. You've heard the songs, right? *Why love don't live here anymore? Love don't love me anymore. What's love got to do with it? I'm a fool in love. Games people play when in love. Love is Sex. Love is Sex in a Jeep. Love is a Jeep.* So, I'm a Jeep now? I guess I'm just another casualty of the deluge of questions and statements that are nothing but a front for the nonsensical madness perpetuated by society's ignorance. That's just a fancy, schmancy, fifty-cent way of saying I've bought the lies. I've drank the Kool-Aid.

My surrender to this distorted view of myself is only made more concrete by the fact I've never known true love. Real love. The kind of love dad says he had with my mother. The one time I came close to it was enough to turn me off forever.

***

Isaiah Johnson liked to be called Ike. Maybe that should have been my clue. In hindsight, he could have very well been Ike Turner, minus the punches of course. No, he never hit me, but if words were blows, then you could call our entire relationship one big TKO.

To all of those whose sight never peered beyond the surface, he was the picture of perfection. And as much as I hate the implications of using food to describe him, it truly is the only way to capture the real flavor of this man. A milk-white smile donned straight teeth set in skin that was a perfect blend of smooth cocoa with a hint of almond.

30

He was one 225lb ball of masculinity wrapped in a shell that screamed confidence. That's the way he walked, too. Is there anything more beautiful than the sensual way a black man moves? The confident sway of intelligence mixed ever so slightly with the jagged edges sharpened by the knives thrown by life. Ike moved differently than any other man I'd seen.

The very scent he left behind when he left a room was intoxicating to anyone who wasn't discerning enough to see past it to the residue of his past. Sadly, I wasn't.

***

It was Deja's fault, my meeting Isaiah. Deja Arnold was my college roommate. We were each other's polar opposite; her being cool and confident and always fabulously coiffed and me being intense and ambitious and well, not so fabulous or coiffed. But, it worked for us. So much so that after "clicking" our freshmen year, we remained roommates all throughout our years at Purdue University. We'd both entered college with an eye towards our future. Strangely, Deja's future always included a man and mine…well, mine never did.

In the spring semester of our sophomore year, Deja became obsessed with online dating. She loved meeting people online. I personally did not understand what she found so intriguing about talking to strangers for months only to meet them in person and discover she'd wasted her time. It was a game to her, and her "adventures" would have been hilarious if it weren't for the fact they were true. Of course as her roommate, she was determined to get me immersed in her world as well.

It wasn't the online part that bothered me really. Everyone does everything online nowadays, so it isn't the taboo it was thirty years ago. It was the dating part that bothered me. I wasn't even sure if I knew what it meant to date. I didn't date much in high school. I attended my senior prom with Jonathan, who just happened to be in between girlfriends and at home from college at the time. So needless to

31

say, with all my teenage angst and mischief, I was still a church girl and my experience with boys was limited.

Another issue that kept me resistant to Deja's repeated requests to venture into the world of cyber dating was more of a personal one. Online dating was just too easy for me. My God, I'm a writer. I like to manipulate words for fun. I could easily become caught up in the "pretending" that is bound to occur when chatting or emailing someone. I knew that, by accident, I'd end up creating a persona that was completely different from who I actually was, and therefore set myself up for more rejection. Even worse, I could end up revealing too much of who I really am, also setting myself up for rebuff.

Deja was very persistent, though. In fact, she went as far as to guarantee me $100 if I didn't meet someone I liked within six months. I kept thinking, *What are you, my pimp? Do I pay* ***you*** *if I do like someone?* But, I kept those thoughts to myself. She did give me her reasoning, though. She said I was boring. All I did was go to class, write in my journal, read my books, and on a rare occasion, attend a frat party or two. Deja's perspective was if I did end up portraying myself differently than who I really was, then maybe I'd be forced to live outside the box. There was nothing, according to her, wrong with that. She was willing to put her money on it.

I have to admit that, back in college, $100 might as well had been $1,000 for a poor student like me. I took that deal with every intention of breezing through the next six months and collecting my money at the end of it all. There was no way I was going to meet anyone anyway, right?

Nineteen-year old college student seeks friendship and more. I am a nice, attractive girl with a decent head on her shoulders and a bright future ahead. Let's talk.

I watched over Deja's shoulder as she typed my description in the online profile.

"You have got to be kidding me," I screeched while lightly pushing her in the back of her head for emphasis.

"What?!"

"You're making me sound like a librarian-in-training."

Okay, I set myself up for that one. Deja looked at me slyly.

"Hey, if the shoe fits…"

"I got your shoe…" I said as I picked up one of my size seven Timbaland boots and threw it at her.

She ducked just in time, all the while laughing.

Feigning hurt, I continued. "Don't guys like for you to put your measurements up there? Why not use one of your old descriptions?" I started singing the old-school, Commodores song my Nana used to sing when I was little and she was feeling herself.

"She's a brick. Hooooouuuuse. She's mighty, mighty. Letting it all hang out."

Deja threw my boot back at me as I continued.

"36-24-36. Ow, what a winning haaaaaand!"

We were both laughing so hard that we bent over holding our stomachs and slapping our knees. Now it was Deja's turn to play hurt.

"Whatever, CJ. I'm not using one of my profile descriptions because you can't handle what comes with that. Don't even front."

This was one of those moments when you are joking around with someone and suddenly something is said that cuts you deeper than a knife ever could. You're not really sure if the stab was intentional or just some remnant of your own subconscious knowledge of yourself, but either way, it hurts like crazy.

"What do you mean, I can't handle it?"

Deja was oblivious to the change in my tone and kept on chuckling.

"Just what I said, girl. Plus, I don't want you to go all Beyonce' your first time out there."

I sat there thinking about how she, and most people, really didn't know me. Even as she continued to write my profile, my mind floated to another place. A point in time that I tried desperately to erase, but could never do so totally.

33

"Hellooooooooo!" Deja was now standing right in front of me and trying to snap me back to the present.

"Okay?" she said

"What?"

"I saaaaaid, let's just put this out there for right now, okay?"

"Whatever," I responded.

She hit send.

***

College was a remarkable time for me. Thanks to Deja and my friends from Chicago, I wasn't totally the wallflower I thought I would be. I partied, protested and prayed with the best of them. Still, there was a part of me that felt different from the others. Holding in pain will do that to you, I guess. It's funny because, growing up, I always wished I could escape the shadow of my mother and, in a way, I was able to do that at college. Nobody knew who Sasha was. Nobody loved her with the passion my father or her friends did. Nobody cared I was her daughter, entering the world just as she was leaving it. And yet, it still didn't feel the way I thought it would—there was no proverbial casting off of chains, most likely because the chains I wore had nothing to do with her. Not really, anyway.

My ideas about God changed in college, also. At least for a little while. For so long, I'd depended—no, counted—on the prayers of my father and grandmother to get me through the tough times. It was like my prayers were always riding shotgun to theirs and I thought they were the only ones who had credibility with the Big Guy. I became comfortable in their vouching for me. But then, it came time to send my prayers up solo. Sometimes, I'd pray about a grade I wanted and other times about friends who were in trouble or about to be in trouble. After countless prayers being answered, I realized that I, too, could ask and receive. This changed the dynamics of my spiritual life, no doubt.

I would later exchange that wonderful and intimate relationship for one that was tangible, yet not nearly as satisfying. Nevertheless, the ease that I felt with God in that

34

first year of school branded His love on my soul, even when I didn't recognize it.

Chapter 4

Four months and one semester had passed since Deja and I made our deal about finding me someone online. I'd gotten some messages from both the weirdest weirdos and some seemingly decent guys. But, I was determined to not let myself become consumed by anyone that reached out to me. It was going to take more than, *"Hey, college girl, what's happening?"* to get my attention. And it did.

I recall sitting in my literature class on one of the milder days in February and getting a text message saying I had a new message from Meetme.com. This was nothing new. Also, nothing new was the fact that I ignored it and continued to listen to a rather captivating presentation on Langston Hughes given by one of the cutest guys in our class. Trust me, it didn't get any better than watching an intelligent and insightful brother who also looked and smelled (hey, he sat in front of me sometimes) good, speak so eloquently about one of your favorite poets—the man who the father you absolutely adored is named after. Mr. Nobody at Meetme.com would surely have to wait.

After the presentation, the professor dismissed the class. I began gathering my books slowly, as I was still moved by the talk and considering how I could incorporate some of the ideas in my writing, when the beauty that was the presenter walked over to me.

"Hey, lady. I see you enjoyed my presentation."

I wasn't quite sure how he knew that, but it didn't matter because I did.

"I did. It was very insightful."

Mr. Beautiful started laughing. I was unnerved because I didn't mean to be humorous.

"Insightful, huh? Yeah, I guess it was."

I began walking towards the door praying that arrogance would not be the reward I'd get for admiring this man. I felt him follow me out of the classroom.

"Nah, I guess I was just hoping for more feedback. You seemed to know a lot about Langston Hughes when we discuss his work in class and I guess I wanted to impress you."

Impress me?

I thought it before I said it.

"Impress me? Why"

He didn't answer me. Unless you call the blinding, white lights of his smile an answer.

"My name is Isaiah."

I just looked at him. He couldn't be hitting on me, could he?

"And your name is Crystal, right?"

I still didn't say anything. I was confused by what was happening. The next thing I know, he smiled again at me and said, what sounded like the strangest thing.

"Would you like to get together and talk about poetry sometime?"

Yeah, right. I can't even see straight when you're talking to me, so how is it we're going to get together and just sit around talking about poetry? This time, I didn't say what I was thinking.

"Sure."

He blinded me again.

"Okay, well, I'll see you in class on Thursday."

And just like that, he was gone.

***

37

So what does this have to do with my Meetme.com experience? Just wait. You'll never believe this in a million years.

I get back to my room and finally decide to check my email. The message left by one interested party, as cryptic as it was, intrigued me greatly.

I was born in the Congo. I walked to the fertile crescent and built the sphinx. I designed a pyramid so tough that a star that only glows every one hundred years falls into the center giving divine perfect light. I am bad.

Ego-trippin. By Nikki Giovanni. There was no picture in his profile and a very vague description, but in his first message...Nikki Giovanni. Hmm. This was one of my favorite poems ever and this guy, this prophet23, sent it as his first message to me. What a wonderful day, I thought. Not only had I been asked out by one of the most intelligent, and as I later found out, popular, guys on campus, but I finally received a message on the site that didn't provoke my gag reflex.

So, I responded accordingly.

I am so perfect so divine so ethereal so surreal. I cannot be comprehended except by my permission. I mean...I...can fly. Like a bird in the sky...

Talk about poetic conversations! I have to admit, I was intrigued by Prophet23. So much so that when Isaiah called the next day for our coffee date, I decided to put him off. Maybe I was crazy, but over the following month, this Prophet23 would have me hooked. We discussed everything from literature to politics, relationships to family with an ease I'd never come across much with "real" guys.

When the time finally came for us to meet, admittedly, I was scared. The beauty of talking online was my insecurities could be carefully hidden in the obscure mechanics of my words. With my words, I was Halle Berry, Oprah Winfrey and

38

Michelle Obama all wrapped up in one grammatically correct email. In person...well, not so much.

The other thing that frightened me was a bit more practical. I knew that meeting this guy would inevitably complicate my life, especially if I liked him. It was easy for me to balance school and work with my cyber dates because I could control the when and what of our conversations. I loved being in control of my romantic life for a change and yet, I knew I would have to relinquish that control once I met the man; saw his face, touched his hand, took in his smile. That was terrifying to me.

At this particular time in my life, I assumed that *whenever* love found me, I would fall hard and fast simply because I yearned for it so much. Therefore, avoiding that path was much easier than traveling it. As I think about it, that was probably why I initially didn't want to pursue anything with Isaiah and found myself avoiding him in class after turning him down for our date. I didn't want to feel obligated to anyone. I didn't know how to be connected to someone without becoming completely absorbed by them. I still don't.

I sat in the coffee shop with my laptop open and my head cocked to one side as I tend to do when I'm writing. I think better that way. The walls in the quaint café located about a mile from campus were painted a royal purple that seemed to soothe and stimulate all at the same time. I'd decided to work on a poem I was writing for my creative writing class, appropriately titled *Is that you, Mr. Livingston?* as I waited for Mr. Meetme.com. While I seemed cool, calm and collected on the outside, I was bubbling with anxiety on the inside. All of the usual questions crossed my mind. What if he was unattractive? What if he thought I was unattractive? What if our chemistry is only electronic and doesn't translate well in real time? Believe it or not, meditating on these questions actually helped me focus on my writing even if the possible answers, to borrow a phrase from my Nana, scared the daylights out of me.

In our last email, I'd told Prophet23 that I'd come to the cafe right after my 4 o'clock class and I'd be wearing a cropped denim jacket and my hair in a high ponytail. I also said I would be seated in the far corner, next to the window on the right side of the door. Fortunately, my class let out a little early, so I was able to get there sooner, make sure I got the right seat and mentally prepare myself for our meeting.

Four o'clock came and went. I didn't see anyone that matched the description Prophet23 gave me and, disappointed, I considered shutting down my computer and leaving. But I really wanted to meet him so, just in case he was running late, I hung around a bit longer.

Still waiting for my date, I did however see walking into the cafe the only person who, in that moment, could make me even more nervous. It wasn't that I didn't *want* to see Isaiah. He was still fine as ever and I still got the chills just from watching him walk. I was just confused as to whether I wanted to see him right then, especially after blowing him off. Realizing I was not going to be able to produce an escape plan in the nanosecond it was going to take for Isaiah to see me sitting at the table, I decided to keep my eyes focused on my screen; faking intense study and hoping he wouldn't come over and try to talk to me.

"So you *do* like coffee?"

So much for that idea.

Lifting my head, I tried my best to act cool, which probably only meant that I wasn't.

"No, I'm a tea girl myself. Hi, Isaiah, what brings you here?"

Suddenly, recognition, as obvious to him as it wasn't to me, spread across his face. I was confused.

"That's funny. I was going to ask you the same thing until..."

Stepping back from the table, his eyes traced my clothes, face and hair, and then he put his hand over his mouth and laughed loudly.

Still confused and a bit anxious at the possibility that my cyber guy would find me smiling uncontrollably with this guy, I responded defensively.

"What's so funny?"

Isaiah stopped laughing and sat down in the chair across from me. His proximity still unnerved me.

"I'm laughing because you...and me, I guess...are SO busted."

Realizing I *still* didn't get it, he smiled that big ole' blinding white smile of his and nearly knocked me off my chair when his voice dropped into its lower register as he stared commandingly into my eyes saying, *"For a birthday present when he was three, I gave my son Hannibal an elephant. He gave me Rome for Mother's Day. My strength flows ever on."*

My heart stopped, if only for one moment, when I realized the implication of his recitation.

"You're Prophet23?" I whispered this as though it were still a secret.

"And I assume you are Chi_gal007," he responded still smiling as though the irony of it all was some great vat of fortune he could wade in for a while.

I, on the other hand, couldn't move. My mind was racing. Every email and every conversation dashed through my head as I realized the man that I could barely bring myself to speak to in class for the past few months was actually the same man I had been sharing my heart with all this time.

"So, how did you do it?"

His face revealed he didn't understand what I meant.

"Do what?"

"Sometimes, in the middle of class, my phone notifies me of new emails from the site. From *you.* How is it possible for you to send me emails when I'm staring at the back of your head in class?"

Isaiah grinned in that way that, even thinking about it now, makes my heart flutter.

"So, you were staring at me?"

If I was lighter, I'm sure my face would have turned several shades of red by then. I didn't mean to imply I was staring at him, even if it was true. His response made me forget he never answered the question.

After getting over the initial shock and embarrassment of it all, Isaiah and I began to talk. In fact, we talked for five hours that day. It was the beginning of something I believed was a divine connection even if, in the end, it was as far away from divine as possible.

***

Our first official date was special. Not because it was traditionally romantic, but because it was romantic in a way that was rather ordinary. Isaiah showed up at my dorm neatly dressed in a button-down shirt that fit just enough to showcase his fit upper body without being too tight and casual pants pressed so well he could slice an apple with their creases. Not to be outdone, I wore my favorite jeans. You know the ones. Every girl has at least one. These jeans fit the curve of my posterior perfectly without crossing the line into hoochie-dom. We stared at one another for a moment and then, he did it again. He smiled.

"You know you have to stop doing that, right," I said jokingly.

"What?"

"Smiling."

"And why is that?" He kept right on smiling as though he knew he was affecting me in a way I had not ever been before.

"Because...because..." I couldn't actually tell him how warm I felt when he smiled, could I?

I gave up. "Just because!"

He started laughing and then suddenly stopped, remembering that it was his smile that caused me this faux frustration. He put on a fake frown, exaggerating his lips by protruding them outward.

I said, "Good. That's better."

But of course by then his sparkling, ecliptic enamels had already rendered me brain dead in one of those moments when the need for companionship outweighs your good sense and you become trapped, hovering anxiously on reality's fine line.

We walked to the movie theater that was located on Main Street. A comfortable silence surrounded us at first and I recalled this was the first time Isaiah, whether online or in person, was quiet. It was okay, though. He held my hand in the chill of the evening and in that, he'd said enough.

After about 15 minutes, Isaiah did finally speak. Stopping and turning toward me, he took my chin between his forefinger and thumb and held it.

"Ms. Germaine, you're looking incredibly beautiful today." He used that same Barry White, Quiet Storm, late-night, dee-jay voice he used in the café to recite poetry.

"Thank you, Isaiah."

"Call me Ike. All of my friends do."

"Okay. Thank you, Ike."

Letting my chin go, we continued walking to the theater.

My mind was lost in his compliment and wondered whether it was a line or if he was being genuine. I'd never considered myself beautiful and I didn't think the stars or moon that shone that night had changed that. Cute? Maybe. Refreshing? Possibly. Clean? Yes. But *incredibly beautiful*? I wasn't too sure about that.

We arrived at the movies and he purchased two tickets. Good. At least he wasn't cheap, I thought. As we walked through the doors, my eyes were drawn to the concession stand marquee that was filled with overpriced soda and popcorn. I saw Ike's eyes on me and for some reason, in that moment, I felt very self-conscious. I really wanted a small popcorn and a box of junior mints, but something about the way he looked at me told me that maybe I should pass. The way he grabbed my hand and pulled me towards our theater confirmed it.

The film, a tear-jerker about a young boy in a Nazi training camp, ended in the most unexpected way and while on any other day I would have mulled over the plot extensively, I could not give it my full attention. I was more captivated by the man who sat beside me. I was awed by the hard way his jaw set as racial epithets were hurled from the screen by the Gestapo. He was fully engaged in the story and I was fully engaged in him.

Leaving the movies, I decided I wanted an Icee. My mouth had dried completely and I needed to swirl something around in it before regular dry mouth became irregular yuck mouth. I didn't want to ruin my chances for a kiss, should there be one. I walked over to the counter and ordered a cherry Icee and as I was walking back to where Isaiah stood, I noticed he'd changed. Disapproval hovered around him like a force field. His body language became harsh, his posture was stiff, and it seemed as if he was angry.

"Is everything alright," I asked, sipping on my drink.

"Fine." His eyes held fast to my cup.

"Would you like some?" He was staring at it so hard, I thought maybe he was thirsty.

His answer was nonverbal. His face twisted in disgust.

"Do you know how much sugar is in those things?"

Actually, I did. But, I also didn't care and I wondered why he did so much.

"Yeah well, I was thirsty." I turned towards the doors signaling we could begin our walk back to my dorm.

He started to say something else. I saw it as plain as if they were my own words. But he didn't and I decided I wasn't going to make a big deal out of his veiled chastisement. So, he didn't like Icees. Okay, I can deal with that. They *aren't* the healthiest things to drink, anyway.

When we passed one of the community garbage cans, I threw the red, white and blue cup into the metal container.

Isaiah looked at me curiously and then grabbed my hand. His smile returned.

***

We had many more wonderfully ordinary dates like that one. Going to the mall or to a campus lecture or to a poetry reading. We also began to travel together. We both were from Chicago. Him, the north side. Me, the south side. So, we both took trips to each other's respective 'hoods. We also went to Cincinnati for the annual Jazz Festival and to Louisville for the Kentucky Derby. They were all good times

44

and with each date, I felt like we were getting closer and closer.

The one thing I loved about him initially was that he never tried to pressure me to have sex. By the time we had been dating three months, I could count on one hand how many times we even found ourselves in a position to contemplate the act. Isaiah seemed to be cool with our abstinence and often said he enjoyed the lovemaking we made with our minds. Boy, did that sound good.

However, I couldn't help to wonder if I was fooling myself by dating Ike. As much as he was handsome and articulate and interesting, I also felt like I was bending over backwards to please him in ways I would probably have never done for anyone else. My reasoning was that, more than liking him as a boyfriend, my heart—the thing that wanted to be needed by someone, the thing that endured the pity of many who saw her as a motherless child—was touched by Ike and the vulnerability that seemed to be right under the surface. He touched me for the first time in a way I'd never been touched. I don't mean sexually, although there was a similar sensuality in the way his soul reached out to mine. There was just this teddy bear-like quality that showed up every now and again in him. It was almost like he knew just when to reveal that little bit to me. He made me think he needed me even when, the longer the relationship lasted, he began to act more like a grizzly bear and I was the one left in need.

I'm sure there were many red flags I missed early on, (like our first date with the Icee), but soon there would be one that was undeniable.

Chapter 5

In the beginning of my junior year, my writing began to really take off. I'd won two poetry contests and one of my short stories was published in a Connecticut literary journal. I was still dating Ike, but as I knew I would, I was becoming consumed by our relationship and my grades from the summer sessions suffered. Writing was the only thing that remained easy.

I entered the new semester determined to be more focused and with a resolve to balance my studies, my writing and my man. Then, however, Ike announced he was running for student government and wanted me to help him with his campaign. My heart sank in defeat. Something was going to have to give and the giving was probably going to have to come from me.

Not that him running for president of SGA was a bad thing. He was a senior and planning to go to grad school at DePaul. He'd even asked me if I could ask my dad to write a recommendation for him. No big deal, I thought. That's what you do in a relationship—you support each other's dreams and goals. It's just that his idea of my helping him would be writing his speeches for him, making flyers and spending any extra time I may have helping him with the campaign. I was torn between making him happy and doing what I needed to do, but there was no way I was going to let him know that. I would just do my best to walk that fine line. He'd win the campaign with my words and maybe, just maybe, I'd still have time to do what I love. Write.

Isaiah's attitude toward my writing was strange to me. When we met, he seemed to love writing. It was the love of great literature that brought us together in the first place. But when it came to my work, he either seemed uninterested or overly critical. I didn't know which was worse: the nonchalant moments when he claimed he had too much on his mind to pay attention or when he did take interest and would rip my writing apart, claiming he was trying to toughen my skin. That was funny because when I challenged him on his work, he was as sensitive as a diaper rash on a newborn.

Ironically, it was this weird back and forth that kept me writing, even if it was the hope of capturing his approval that drove me most of the time. Born from one of his mean-spirited critiques was the short story that won the Connecticut Review contest and the one that the dean of the English department asked me to present in an off-campus discussion on modern creative writing followed by a Q&A.

So, it was my time to shine. I was so excited because for the first time, I would actually be presenting my work to an audience instead of just my friends and the random person who happened to be sitting next to me at the café. I knew there would be constructive criticism and I felt like whatever was said, I could handle it because it would only make me a better writer.

The day I was scheduled to give my reading, Ike was supposed to pick me up and take me to the off-campus lecture hall on the other side of town. The reading was scheduled for 5pm, so I wanted to get there early, around 4:15, so I could pray and get my mind right before I went on. Well, at 4:15, Ike was nowhere to be found. I tried calling and texting him, and he didn't answer. By 4:30, my patience had worn thin and I decided to call Deja to see if she could drop me off. Fortunately, she was still in our room. She threw on some clothes, ran downstairs and we jumped in her car. Of course, two minutes after we pull off, my phone rings.

47

"Where are you?"

I know he's not screaming at me.

"No, the question is, where *were* you," I said this as tersely as I could possibly muster without encouraging my often-boisterous roommate's sistergirl background commentary. "I told you that I needed to be there at 4:15pm. I waited for you in the lobby of my dorm for a half hour."

"And I told *you* I had a meeting and I would come afterwards. The meeting ran over. Why does it matter anyway? The show doesn't start till five."

I wanted to say that he didn't have the right to make assumptions about what mattered or not when it came to me, but I didn't. I didn't want to argue with him about this, especially before one of the most exciting days of my life.

"That's fine."

"So?"

"So, what?"

"Where are you?"

Unbelievable, right?

"I'm almost at Beacon Hall. Did you really think I was going to wait on you and be late?"

His silence seemed odd.

"Yes, I did." He finally said. "So who took you?"

"Deja."

"Sure she did."

This was interesting to me because Ike had never acted even remotely jealous before and now his tone seemed to imply he didn't believe Deja had driven me.

"Listen, I'm here now. I want to go in and get settled. If you're still coming..."

Click.

"Hello?"

Silence.

"Hello?"

Busy signal.

He'd hung up on me. I'll deal with him when I get home later, I thought.

I should have known better.

48

The presentation itself went great. As I read, I sensed the engagement of the audience from beginning to end. My words seemed to pull them into both the tragedies and triumphs that befell the characters in my story. It was fascinating. Following the reading, I opened the floor for questions.

"Are any of the characters based off of real people," a short, red-haired man with Harry Potter spectacles asked.

I knew that one was coming.

"Well, while none of these characters are real, there are many aspects to their personalities that I've picked up from observing the people closest to me. Mr. Jessie is a lot like my father in the way he carries himself and Lacey's attitude probably mirrors my roommate a bit. Sorry, Deja."

Deja, who sat on the edge of the semicircle that formed the audience, rolled her eyes and then smiled. "No problem, roomie."

Everyone laughed.

The other questions that were asked were typical ones about how long it took me to write the story, plot structure and character development. For the most part, people seemed to either enjoy the reading or, at the very least, were other local writers who were curious about the process. I was feeling pretty good with the entire event when the final question was asked.

"Crystal..." he said with a strange mix of familiarity and disdain.

"...the story, to me, seemed a bit amateurish. The characters were rather flat, including Mr. Jessie who could have used more depth and detail. The ending left me hanging with a weird taste in my mouth, as if I'd eaten something that started off tasting pretty good, but then gradually turned sour with every chew."

There were a few chuckles from the room as everyone turned their heads to see who uttered the scathing critique. Of course, I already knew who it was. I was stunned. Even worse, the balminess of embarrassment spread from the top of my head down to my shoes and my mind scrambled for a response.

"Thank you very much, Isaiah, for that...*constructive*...critique. I'll definitely make note of it. While I disagree with parts of your feedback, I will admit that you are right about one thing. I am an amateur. That's something I'm proud of because that means I'm always growing."

I ended the reading right after that and hurried to the back room before the tears that had begun to well in my eyes became evidence of my hurt. Deja quickly followed behind me.

"How could he?" I said.

I guess she had no words that could possibly render a plausible explanation because she just grabbed my coat and book bag and led me to the door as I kept my head down.

"What the –?"

Without looking up at all, I knew what caused her to nearly curse.

"Hey, baby..." Ike said, hugging me as if he hadn't verbally ripped my writing (and my heart) to shreds just a few moments before. Deja looked like she was ready to box as I looked over his shoulder at her twisted face. He finally put me down. "Why, Ike?"

"Why what?"

Deja started towards him as though she wanted to help him to remember. Boy, was she tough! I put my hand up to stop her.

"Why did you say what you said out there? I thought you were here to support me."

"I am supporting you. I'm here, right?"

I noticed he still hadn't said "good job." Maybe I didn't do as well as I thought I did. I think that was the first time I actually thought I heard the surface of my confidence crack.

"Yes, and I'm glad you are here..."

I heard Deja suck her teeth in the corner.

"...but..."

"But what? You can't handle a little criticism?"

"Yes, I can handle *a little* criticism, but why did you have to be so mean?"

"You call that mean? Those comments were to make you better. A great writer knows how to handle constructive criticism."

I thought Deja was going to come out of her skin on that one.

"I guess I'm not a great writer then!"

I said that with part sarcasm and part expectation because I knew I was good, maybe not great, but definitely good. And I guess I just wanted him to say it.

"No, not great dear. But, don't worry. I'm here to help you." He switched on his 100-watt smile and slowly took my coat and bag away from Deja, who was now about to burst if she didn't say anything.

"And here I thought he was here to love you! Silly me."

Her comment of course didn't phase Ike. In fact, he was probably impressed by her analysis of his intentions, whereas I just chose to believe that maybe I'd gotten it wrong this time. This would not be the first time I saw — and ignored — the shadow that hung over his soul. Admittedly though, the light that drew me to him became a little dimmer after that day. Only I had no idea what to do about it.

***

I did, however, learn something about Ike and myself that day. This man carried himself with an elegance that belied his years and with an intelligence that could captivate both the simple and the wise. That way of being is what drove his popularity. Yet, in the face of all of that good, there was plenty bad. He was insecure and, I'd later find out, a little bit emotionally unstable. The bad thing was, I think he knew it. Even worse, I knew it. But, I guess in some way, I thought I could help him.

I became what I would eventually abhor in other Christian women — masking the very-real shortcomings of a man by telling themselves he was some kind of divine assignment. Accepting certain immaturity in exchange for potential growth and never fully seeing any fruits of their labor. If I'm honest, I believed Ike was my God-ordained mission project. The one I was going to save. The one I was going to change. Every clue I was given that he wasn't mine to save was lost in his ability to manipulate me into giving more and more to him without any regard to myself. His manipulation kept me confused about his true intentions, and the inner conflict that seemed to brew just below the surface of his cool swagger and charm never revealed itself through intimacy, but often through fits of anger or degradation.

***

I couldn't help it. I thought if I had sex with him, maybe I could break through the wall that seemed to go up whenever we'd get close. I know, I know. Beyond the obvious implications, that has to be the worse thing a girl can do. But truthfully, I was desperate. When we first met, this man showed me so much attention; attention that I thought I needed. Everyone on campus knew we were an item and I kind of liked the fact that his popularity became mine by association, even if I was put off by the phoniness of it all. However, in our quiet times, when he was lying across my bed in my dorm room or we were sitting across from each other at the café, the air felt stagnant between us. Whenever I tried to extend our conversation beyond poetry and politics, I felt like I was in a tug-of-war with a lion. So, knowing the power of sex and the emotional bond that it could create between us...good or bad...I thought I'd try to save our relationship that way. It was a disaster.

Isaiah walked into his room and although he seemed surprised to find me there, a quick look around told him exactly what was up. Six large candles were lit and positioned around the room, each one representing the six months we'd officially been exclusively dating. I stood there, hair freshly braided in the micro style I knew he liked, dressed in a gold, silk nightgown and robe I'd borrowed from Deja. When he beamed at me with that smile of his, my heart began to race and fear seeped into my soul. I was torn. My body wanted him, but I couldn't shake the feeling that something was off. I didn't think I could just blow out the candles, grab my coat and leave without some type of confrontation, so I told myself, and God I think, that even if this is wrong, it was for the greater good. I was doing it for him.

He put his book bag down and walked over to me. Wrapping his arms around me, I felt the coolness that he wore like a badge of honor slowly melt away as he stroked my back and lightly ran his hands through the back of my hair. In that moment, I felt beautiful and was willing to give him my all.

We moved towards the makeshift queen-sized bed that really was two twin beds pushed together, and laid down. I shook with a combination of anxiety and anticipation as he removed his shirt and began to kiss me softly and then a little bit more aggressively on the lips. The temperature of the room seemed to climb a hundred degrees.

"Kiss me here," he said pointing to his chest. I did.

"Not like that..." Isaiah tore the top part of the borrowed gown. "...like this."

He kissed me with full lips, which felt really good, until he ended the kiss with a bite. Not a soft, tender, playful bite either. This was a "boy does this apple taste good" kind of chop.

"Ow!" He didn't seem to hear me or feel me jerk.

"Kiss me like that," he said again, a little louder, still pointing at his chest.

With teeth prints in my breast, I still tried to kiss him the way he wanted, but I couldn't bring myself to bite him the way he'd bitten me.

"What are you doing?"

Isaiah held my wrists, pushing me away from him with a look of disgust on his face.

My heart wrenched as I sat up and moved to the edge of the bed. What had I done? All I wanted to do was show him that it was okay to open up and love me, and yet in doing that, I'd somehow tapped into some weird proclivity of his.

"I should have known you weren't ready." He said this as he blew out the candles, gathered my bag and shoes, and practically pushed me out the door. Standing in the hallway, I was in total shock. *Did this just happen*, I thought. I knocked on the door because he'd forgotten to give me my coat and he opened it, threw the coat at me, and slammed the door shut in my face. Everything happened so fast. I put the coat on over the torn nightgown (thank God it was a trench coat) slid on my shoes and made my way back to my dorm. The tears danced freely across my face nearly crystallizing in the cold February air.

He was right about one thing. I wasn't ready. It was the rejection of all rejections. And in spite of it all, I wasn't ready to leave him either. But, in all the craziness, I did feel like I was ready to leave school. Not over this one incident, but over all the incidents I knew were to come. It had become too much for me. I figured I'd sit out the spring semester and focus on my writing. Isaiah would graduate in May and then I could return in the fall. Without him on campus, I could focus better. Can you believe that all of this made perfect sense to me? The worst part is that I kept my "sabbatical" from my father by staying with a friend in Indiana and changing my address on all of my records. Dad paid my tuition for the entire year in the fall, so he wouldn't suspect a thing.

Isaiah and I never revisited the sex issue again, but remained together as pseudo-boyfriend and girlfriend. As weeks went by, I never knew what to expect from Ike. There were days I truly believed we had a chance because he was so sweet and nice. There were other days he'd literally become unrecognizable as his monster tongue would unleash all kinds of madness or he'd find the most awful ways to shut me out by making me feel less than human, or at least less than him. Even so, I had high expectations of him and I think that was the reason it took me so long to break away.

Chapter 6

As I navigated my tumultuous relationship with Ike, I began to question love even more. I'd never really considered it a real option until I'd met him and I had no point of reference of what I was supposed to do or how I was supposed to act while in love. Maybe I was doing something wrong, I thought. So I went to the wisest woman I knew and asked her what it meant to be in love.

"Hey, Nana!" I bounced into the room that hadn't changed in 20 years, thinking about how good it always felt to go to my grandmother's house. Even when I was a little girl, I was always soothed by the scents and sounds that came from that quaint three-bedroom townhouse on Woodlawn Avenue. Nana turned around slowly with a huge grin on her face.

"That's my baby! Come here and give this old lady a kiss."

As my lips touched the side of her face, smooth compared to other 72-year-old women, I made a loud smacking sound that came more from the back of my teeth than my lips.

"There you go with that ole' fake mess. You better give me some sugar right."

That was a joke between us. I know it may sound weird, but when I was a child, I didn't know how to kiss. Don't laugh. Whenever someone would lean in to get some "sugar," I would pucker my lips and bump their face. No kissing sound, just skin to skin. It frustrated me that my kisses never made the sound like other people's, and so I decided to take my tongue and rub it against my teeth in order to recreate the sound. I didn't realize that the lips actually made the kissing sound all by themselves when you opened and close them until my Nana gave me a "sugar" lesson at eight years old. From then on, I would always give her my fake kiss first and then follow up with a real one. She loved it.

That day, Nana was cooking. She was leaning over a bucket in the kitchen snapping beans. I stared at her with a smirk on my face.

"You know you can buy them already snapped, Nana."

She stopped and looked at me with a frown. I always liked to mess with her and her old-fashioned ways.

"And how do I know who snapped 'em?"

I just laughed. Some things never changed and I'm glad.

"Whatchu' doing home, girl? Something must be on your mind."

Nana always seemed to know when I needed to talk. Sometimes when I felt overwhelmed, I'd come to Chicago and see her and not even tell my dad I was in town. She would always keep my secret.

"I want to know about love."

"Jesus is love."

Nana looked up at me with a sly smile on her face. I wasn't the only one who liked to mess with people. I got it honestly.

"Stop, Nana." I whined. "You know what I'm talking about. I know about Agape, Phileo and Eros, and all that stuff you learn at church. I'm talking about the how's and why's of it. When you fell in love with Granddad, how did you know what to do? I need to know how and why to love."

56

Nana stopped snapping the beans, moving the bucket to the other side of her chair. She then took her cane that was leaning against the cabinet and began walking out of the kitchen and into the living room. I knew to just follow her while she thought about her answer.

Sitting in her favorite velvet, winged-back chair, she told me to sit on the matching ottoman in front of her. I could tell from the look in her eyes that one of those "memories of Sasha" flashed in front of her. I needed an answer, so I chose to not say anything about that and I'm glad she didn't, either.

"What's his name?"

"Huh?"

She just looked at me. I knew what she was asking me.

"His name is Isaiah."

"*Aaaah, The Lord is generous. Salvation of the Lord. God's helper.*"

I think Nana knew the meaning of everyone's name, including mine. Crystal Justine: *Follower of Christ. Just and Upright.*

"Loving someone is a choice, CJ. It's not something that you fall into and it's not always something that's fated. I know it's easier to stay with someone because you think that God divinely brought you together, but that is not always the case. Sometimes God brings someone into your life for just a moment, to teach you something, and after you learn it, you are supposed to move on. But sometimes we cling to the temporary and shun the permanent. I can only imagine that that frustrates Him."

I knew that Nana was reaching far back into her mind, recalling memories of long ago. There was no way that I could know the magnitude of what she was sharing. Not now anyway.

"Okay. So say I choose to love someone. How do I do that? How much should I take from that person before I decide that maybe I shouldn't love them anymore?"

That's how foreign love...this kind of love...was for me. I was calculating it. I was clocking the time spent, effort invested. I was seeing it the wrong way. Nana made sure that she told me that, too.

"How much you should *take* from someone? You shouldn't be *taking* anything from him."

She paused as another memory took shape on her face and in her mind. I don't know if she misunderstood what I meant by *take* or if this was just her way of teaching me something else.

"Love is about giving. It's sacrificial at its very core. In the love you and I share, we give support and understanding, time and comfort. We also challenge each other. That's a form of giving, too."

It seemed like too much to me.

"The question you should be asking yourself, CJ, is how much of all those things can you...should you...be giving this man? And has he shown you he is willing to give them to you?"

I knew the answer to at least one of those questions.

***

The final straw was at the end of that school year. Isaiah was graduating and I'd spent the entire semester dodging my father, trying to write something meaningful and helping Isaiah get into grad school. It was a catch 22 for me because he kept pressing about my dad's recommendation letter to DePaul and I was trying to keep any talk of college with my dad to a minimum, lest the fact that I wasn't in school should come up. That didn't matter to him, of course. Never one to be put off, Ike kept pressing me for the letter, even after the semester ended. It wasn't that he really needed the letter because he'd already been accepted into the program. For him, it was about the prestige of having one of the most distinguished professors in the school endorse him. Plus, the support of Langston Germaine was a great thing for his file and his resume, and I even knew that.

Still, there was something inside of me that didn't feel good about it. A gnawing feeling had settled in my gut even as I was writing the glowing recommendation for him and

58

having my dad sign it. That uneasiness took a backseat, per usual, as I figured that doing this for him couldn't hurt our relationship, but only help it. And the lack of closeness, the constant criticism, even the desire for the intrigue of friendship that we had in the very beginning, made me desperate to do anything.

That June, Ike had moved back to the North side of Chicago, this time into a studio apartment on Fullerton Ave near the DePaul campus. I also moved back to Chicago and back with my dad. I was careful to pretend that the semester had gone well, not letting my "hiatus" leak out.

Excited to be back in the city, I decided to deliver my dad's letter to Ike personally by surprising him at his place. I even thought maybe I'd give the whole sex thing another try, just in a more low-key, less-dramatic manner. I felt like I had to do something because the way things had been going, I was grasping at straws trying to close the distance that had grown between us. Like my roommate Deja used to say, I needed some glue to keep this thing together and although back then I chastised her for equating the beauty of love making to the white stuff made by Elmer, I'd secretly decided to give it a shot. As scary as the thought is to me now, back then I'd reconciled I would do *whatever* he wanted.

After exiting the Red Line train and walking two blocks west, I finally came upon Isaiah's apartment. My heart beat loudly in my ears. I knocked on the door and waited. He answered with a smile.

"Hey, you!" The sound in his voice said he was glad to see me.

"Surprise, baby!"

He gave me his trademark smile and I felt the warmth I'd missed for so long. I walked into the apartment and was surprised by how impeccably neat and well-designed it was. His college apartment was always a mess.

"Your apartment looks fabulous. If I was a jealous girl, I'd think you had some other woman over here to hook it up." I looked at him hopeful.

He just continued to smile and then said, "I can promise you that *this* is not the work of another woman. You are the only woman in my life, dear."

I was pleased to hear it.

I could tell that he was anxious, but I thought maybe he'd sensed I wanted to try again at taking our relationship to another level. That wasn't it at all.

"Do you have something for me," he said.

Thinking we were on the same page, I reached in my bag and pulled out a black and red teddy and a condom.

"I sure do, sweetie."

He looked back and forth between me and my "gifts" and his whole body, face included, reflected an immediate transformation in mood and disposition. In hindsight, I wish I could have seen it in slow motion because I'm sure he could have given the Hulk a run for his money.

More than a physical change, his voice seemed to change into something near diabolical. Low, deep and cryptically slow. "I'm so sick of this. I'm so sick of you."

Talk about confused. I don't know why I didn't get it. I don't know if my need to be loved distorted my intelligence or if I simply chose to not see it.

"What's wrong, Ike? I just thought we could..."

He cut me off by screaming, "...could what!?"

I didn't know what to say. My head was pounding as every emotion known to man fought its way to the surface. Anger won.

"You're sick of me? *Really*, Isaiah?"

The shadow I'd seen hovering over his soul now seemed to envelope mine with a totality that prevented me to have any control over my words.

"I'm the one who should be sick! You approached *me*, remember? And yet you have the nerve to tell me you're tired of me when you've been nothing but a selfish and disturbed, little man who feels the need to bring other people down in order to build himself up. I don't even know why I put up with you and your stank attitude for as long as I have!"

My head was now throbbing as I struggled to breathe under the weight of my pent up frustrations. In the midst of my tirade, Isaiah smiled and for the first time, I saw the wickedness that lied in those pearly whites.

"Oh *you know* why you put up with me for as long as you have. Because you had no choice. You're nothing without me and I saw it from the very beginning. A sad, little girl seeking the love she never got from her dead mommy. Baby, you were my most perfect challenge. Book smart, but weak. Time and time again you proved you weren't worth pursuing anything real with because you couldn't even stand up for yourself when it counted."

My stomach convulsed as he continued to talk. I could have sworn I was speaking to the devil himself.

"Yeah, I approached you. Even online, I knew it was you. Remember those emails you got in the middle of class? All planned out. I had a purpose, dear. All that time, you were trying hard to get me to open up, trying to 'help' me, and I played right along, knowing full well you didn't know what you were talking about. Me, on the other hand, knew exactly what I wanted and *exactly* how to get it."

He paused and looked down at my bag that had fallen to the floor.

"I think you have something for me?"

The letter. He'd planned it all along. He never had any intention of really being with me. Someone had told him who my father was and he'd concocted a plan that would help him further his career.

I exploded. "Do you honestly think I would give you the letter after what you have done to me!?"

"First of all, I did nothing to you. You did it to yourself. If you were stupid enough to believe *I* would really be interested in someone like *you*, then that's your own fault. Secondly, if you don't want dear ole' dad to find out you dropped out last semester without telling him, I'd hand over the letter."

What could I do? I reached in my bag and pulled out the envelope. In my heart, what was left of it, I wanted to rip

61

the letter to shreds, showing him that his plan, however well played, didn't work out in the end. But my mind rationalized by doing that, I would be risking the love and approval of the only man I knew loved me for sure. I handed the letter to the snake I used to call boyfriend.

Isaiah grabbed the letter and opened it, reading it right there in front of me. For a fleeting moment, I thought maybe in this terrible nightmare, I'd finally get the approval of my writing I so desperately sought from him. But I didn't. He just put the letter back in the envelope and turned away. I was dismissed.

As I walked to the door, Isaiah called my name. I'm not proud to say it, but hope still found its way to my eyes as I turned back to him. Unfortunately, he just handed me the lingerie that had fallen out of my hands and with that wicked grin, broke even more heartbreaking news.

"By the way, the sex would not have been very good. I'm gay. Always have been. You do make a fabulous cover, though."

Thinking I might pass out, I ran out the door.

***

When it was all said and done, I felt rotten on the inside. As though my heart had been ripped from my chest cavity and chewed into a million pieces by Isaiah the Cannibal. Like he then spit it out and steamrolled the remains with a combination of pain and anguish. I know it sounds dramatic, but that's the way it felt.

The pastor at my father's church used to always say "hurt people, hurt people." But this was more than hurt. I was emotionally stunted by Ike's interruption in my life. Months later, even as I tried to regain what was taken away from me, I would find myself crying tears of crocodile proportions. Then I'd think, maybe he didn't take anything from me. Maybe I gave it away. It's beyond frustrating to try to regain a self-esteem that took years to build and only a few seconds, and a few words from one man, to lose.

I hate to say this because I've read enough books to know how it sounds. But I sometimes think I must have been crazy to believe I could be loved. I got caught up with Ike and believed the hype. I let that small glimmer of hope hold me captive. Even thinking about it reminds me that my wall must remain firmly in place, if I want to stay safe. I can't let the depression take over. I can't allow myself to go to that place again. I can't let anyone or anything have that much control over my emotions again. It's a horrific feeling to know that one man can shatter your world.

With his rejection, I'd changed from being a smart, talented and *on my good days*, beautiful woman to an insecure, weak, needy girl. I HATED that. I tried to keep it together, but absolutely despised the fact that I let myself fall apart in the first place.

Yet, all in all, I also know that my relationship with Isaiah was somewhat of a big self-fulfilling prophecy. He was the mirror image of what was going on with me emotionally and spiritually. I didn't have authentic self-esteem because I'd placed too much value on being in this relationship with him. Everyone else could see that but me. I'd subconsciously believed that without the love and attention of this particular man, I wasn't worth much, and therefore, I was treated that way. I was skeptical of his actions and words whenever he was not with me and viewed everything he did for himself as an act against the relationship and ultimately against me. Therefore, it ended up exactly as I thought it would.

Growing up, I used to hear the old ladies at church say all the time, "The devil is a liar." Well, they couldn't have been more right. Unfortunately, what they should have said was that although he is a liar, the devil is also charming, sexy and intriguing. And that he stood about six feet four inches tall with a baldhead and perfect, pearly whites. I did mention his teeth, didn't I? More like fangs to me now. At least *then* I would have recognized the devil when he showed up in my life. Nope. Nobody told me that. I guess it would have been just too easy that way. Nonetheless, Isaiah was my first, and what I hope to be last, bout with love.

63

Chapter 7

I've been told that I will always remember with fondness the lean years of my writing career. Right. I'd actually prefer not. The people who say that are the same people who recite that old cliché about whatever didn't kill me would make me stronger. I'm thinking, if I'm never pushed to the brink of death in order to be able to say that I was stronger, that would be quite alright with me. I don't know if it's worth all that. In a way, I understand what they're trying to say. I've pushed myself through times of lack and writer's block by reciting those exact same clichés. Nevertheless, I've also learned the term "starving artist" is not as much of a badge of honor, as some of my writer friends have convinced themselves.

At first, I didn't like writing too much. I felt like it forced a transparency I wasn't really ready to give. But then, I learned how to manipulate words so they mean only what I want them to mean. Some of my critics say that's the problem with my writing. That it feels like I manufacture emotions instead of allowing them to flow freely. Well, I say that *most* people aren't critics and so *most* people don't know that. *Most* people read honestly, even if I don't always write honestly.

I think I've always known I would be a writer, even when I didn't want to pursue it. After the Ike "incident," I returned to Purdue and finished my degree in Journalism/Mass Communication. In my senior year, I interned at various local publications and took free writing gigs in order to prove to myself I could actually cut it. I was fortunate enough to have a father who invested in the pursuit of my dream while I was in school. After the Bank of Daddy closed shop, I worked various nondescript jobs to pay for my laptop, my tiny apartment on Cottage Grove and the various writing conferences and workshops I attended. However, when the paychecks got smaller and bill collectors began to call incessantly, I realized this was not, could not be, a game I'd chosen, but rather a purpose in life. It had to be, if I was going to risk having absolutely nothing to be good at it. As soon as I began to change the way I thought about writing, that's when the opportunities started to come.

***

I took my first full-time writing gig at a small, weekly newspaper. No, it wasn't exactly what I wanted to be doing, but it kept me working in my field, which was most important to me at that time. To tell the truth, there wasn't much real writing to it. I spent most of the time re-writing press releases about local events. The few chances I did get to write something else were usually local human-interest stories. Unfortunately, the humans were rarely all that interesting. After a few short months of "getting my feet wet," I started to feel stifled. Like I was choking on some angelic AP Manual unable to really explore the outer realms of the rules. I understood that newspaper journalism was a good start, but truthfully, I needed more creative freedom. I needed to feel like I wasn't just informing people, but moving them. Inspiring them. That's where the whole book idea came from.

I want to write a story that keeps the reader engaged from beginning to end. One of the strong points of my writing is my ability to use language like a cinematographer uses film — to paint a picture in the mind's eye that's vivid and arresting. The first thing every writer learns is to show more than you tell. I believe that wholeheartedly, but I also think you have to go so much deeper than that.

Writing is the only place where people truly understand me. Not just know me, but understand me. There is a difference, you know. My Nana says all the time, "Knowledge is the acquisition of information. Wisdom is understanding that information and placing it in the proper context, giving it a purpose." At the newspaper, I give my readers knowledge. I inform them of what's going on in our community and tell them a little bit about the people who they call neighbor. But there's more to what I do than that.

Colors reach out to me from the canvas of my mind. The purple splashes of my inner queen speaks loudly and almost brazenly to the cool blue of my inner peace. Red dances seductively to the calypso beat of my heart and yellow shines brightly, overcoming even my greenest days.

That's what I'm talking about! It's not that I mind writing what I call the "straight" stuff because it pays the bills and buys me some time, but this is the kind of stuff I'm really drawn to writing. I had it all wrong in the beginning. It's actually safer writing creative non-fiction or even fiction. Like I said before, I can move people with that kind of writing. Even in fiction, I can become a manipulator of emotions, twisting my characters to fit the emotional response I want to invoke in the readers. I'll admit it's more than just the style of writing that intrigues me. It's the control. That kind of control, even if it's within the context of a story, is weirdly satisfying.

Jonathan, my best friend, says I need to be careful. He has told me more than once, "That's all fine and good when you're making up stories, but don't let it trickle into real life. Your need to control people like your characters is a surefire way to become the source of your own heartache." I guess he thinks the desire for control will cause me to end up doing some emotional manipulation in reality. That ship has already sailed, unfortunately. I've perfected that skill. It's the only way to not hurt.

Jonathan also says I should go ahead and write my book now. I can just hear him. "What are you waiting for, CJ?"

A reasonable question, I suppose. I think I'm waiting for "my moment." I think there's a time in a writer's life after they've studied the craft enough and practiced their craft enough when a moment comes along that changes their writing destiny. I'm still too green right now, but I know the moment is coming soon. In fact, the call I received a few months ago was just the beginning, I think.

The ring tone on my cell blared loudly in the middle of the restaurant where Jonathan and I were having lunch. I was annoyed by the women who were batting their eyes at him as though he wasn't sitting there with me, a woman. Did they think I wasn't good enough to be with someone like him? Probably. We were just friends, but I'm not blind. Jonathan has always been uber-gorgeous with his rich, mahogany skin, and beautiful lips and teeth. Anyway, I was still a bit perturbed at the assumption of these anonymous women when I picked up the phone.

"Hello?"

Now it was Jonathan's turn to feel insecure. He hated when I answered the phone while we were hanging out.

He said, "You're too old to have such an obnoxious ringer."

"Shut up," I mouthed back at him.

The unrecognizable voice on the other end spoke with an accent that had that Chicago-by-way-of-the-Bronx flavor. "Is this Crystal Germaine?"

"Who's calling?" I had had my share of bill collectors call to know that you never agree to your identity until you're sure of who's calling. Of course, Jonathan finds this hilarious and bursts out laughing.

"Hi, this is George at *Epic Magazine*. Is this Cris?"

My first thought was of how arrogant it was for this *George* to assume he could shorten my name. But then, I realized he'd said he was from *Epic Magazine*. I had just queried them an article a couple of weeks before. I smiled this huge grin at Jonathan, whose curiosity overcame the pretend jealousy he'd displayed before.

"This is she."

"We received your query and article submission, and we're interested in using it for an upcoming issue."

Yeaa! Boy, was I happy. Another great clip. I wasn't prepared for the next thing he said.

"As a matter of fact, we were wondering if you were interested in a staff position with us in our Chicago office?"

"Wow. A staff position? That sounds great."

Jonathan's full lips released the pearly whites that were held captive by their size, stretching from ear to ear as he realized what was happening. I absolutely love that he is always genuinely happy for me.

"Yeah, we really like your voice and could use someone like you in our Midwest office. When I get back from New York, I'll set up a meeting with you to discuss the details."

"Sounds good. I look forward to meeting you."

"Ditto." Click.

That was it. That's how it happened. Short and sweet and very much real. It wasn't *the* moment, but it was quite possibly the moment before *the moment*. Of course, I screamed and cried and all that good stuff. I declared to Jonathan, *as though he wasn't right there when it happened,* that *Epic Magazine,* one of the top lifestyle publications in America, wanted to hire me as a staff writer. He reflected back to me the joy I felt by the way he beamed at me the rest of the day. I called my dad, Nana and my aunts. I knew they all would be proud of me. For the first time in a very long time, I was proud of me.

***

One year later and I found myself right smack in the middle of a major writer's block. Once I'd gotten established at *Epic,* moving up to junior editor in six months, I'd decided to go ahead and give my book a shot. I think it was mostly fear. People were beginning to know my name now. In addition to the magazine, I had my own blog with a decent following and had even dabbled a bit in political commentary. Yet, there was something way down deep inside of me that had, for the previous few weeks, prevented me from picking up a pen (or laptop) and writing anything that could even remotely be considered a book. I actually think I would be lying by calling it block. A block seems to imply there is something other than me standing in the way of all the creativity that has been near boiling point in my brain. If that was the case, then I wouldn't be able to write at all. No, it definitely wasn't a block. Blaming it on the devil would've been too easy and quite frankly, giving him too much credit.

It's more like, I cannot turn my brain off, no matter how much I try. Thoughts upon thoughts constantly race through my mind. One minute I might be thinking about the book and the next, I might be thinking about work or my latest bootleg romance. And still the next minute, I'm thinking about what I need to do next week, next month and next year, simultaneously. Even more ridiculous, I'd found myself thinking about thinking. This is, of course, just a nice way of saying I was severely distracted. Even I knew this was madness. And more and more, I began to feel like such madness was beyond just unsatisfactory. It was a slap in the face of the One who has so mercifully gifted me to write. The truth was, I'd allowed the critic in my own head to go beyond simply challenging me to be better. I'd allowed that critic to buy space in my head she was only supposed to lease.

I'd always envied those who knew how to turn everything off and calmly focus. The disciplined folk. Not me. When it came to writing the book, something that was such a great desire in my heart, I couldn't get out of my own way. So, I stopped altogether. I put the book aside and figured maybe it wasn't time.

Chapter 8

What do you do when you pray and pray, and God doesn't answer you? Some say that even then, He's answering. I don't know if I believe that. I think sometimes He leaves things for us to figure out on our own.

When I consider my faith and how it has changed over the years, I think back to one day in particular, when I was 11 years old and sat in Mt. Moriah Baptist Church with my father and grandmother. This had to be one of those special days, maybe even a church anniversary or something, when youth church was cancelled. Usually, my attention span would only allow me to catch about five minutes of the sermon before my mind turned toward the seemingly more important subjects of my burgeoning adolescence: school, friends, books and boys. However, that day, actually two weeks after my eleventh birthday, I heard the words whispered softly I'd been longing to hear for as long as I could remember.

You are SO special to me.

At first, I thought my dad was speaking to me, but when I looked up at him, his eyes were closed and his mouth was shut. I then turned to my Nana who sat on the other side of me, and while her mouth was moving, I could tell she was immersed in prayer and not speaking to me. Then, I heard it again.

You are SO special to me.

It wasn't an audible voice, but it wasn't the "head" voice I'd become familiar with, either. It was something else altogether. My child-self knew not to be afraid and because I didn't fear, a warmth that began at the center of my chest spread throughout my body like someone was filling me up with new blood. I knew who it was. It was Jesus and He loved me. Even at eleven, I somehow knew God had spoken to me and this sent me skipping down the aisle when the preacher made the call. Yes, skipping! Members of my church still remind me of how funny it was to see this little girl skipping down to the altar and I'll admit, if I saw that today, I'd laugh, too. But to me, it was the most natural thing to do. When I was little, I skipped when I was happy. I skipped when I was excited to be playing. And this was no different. I was so glad to meet Jesus. I was so glad He thought I was special.

Following my salvation, my enthusiasm over this new relationship translated into me writing plays and making up songs about Him. I wanted to know as much as my young mind could hold about Him because I somehow felt (though unable to fully articulate) He was my ticket away from the pain I'd seen reflected in my father's eyes or the faces that seemed to look upon our family with more pity than love.

It's too bad I'm now so far removed from the spiritual elation that resonated so powerfully to me as a child. Today, I long for those feelings of trust and confidence and peace and the purest of joys. Now, my faith is more vanilla than anything. Ordinary. Built upon the basics with no expectation of miracles or sometimes, even the run-of-the-mill blessings. The child-like thrill of knowing God has all but dissolved as His voice has become lost in the sea of other voices that crowd my head. I don't skip to God anymore, if you know what I mean. It's more of a slow, painful stagger, aided by the life-induced crutches of my own creation.

***

Out of all of my mother's best friends, I'm the closest to Kara. She's been Aunt Kara to me since I was born. She's also married to my father's best friend, Uncle Benson. I can't stand him. I *really* can't stand him. Sometimes I feel guilty about that whenever I'm talking to her because she has been so sweet to me over the years. I don't deserve her kindness and yet I keep coming back for more, and she keeps pouring in to me. Aunt Kara is the one who taught me how to pray. I mean, really pray. Not the "God is good, God is great" that my dad taught me when I was a toddler. In her typical old-school Pentecostal fashion, she taught me how to "plead the Blood" and "intercede." I must admit, even though I consider myself a little bit more of an evolved, progressive Christian, when things get ugly, as they so often do, I still know how to get it in if necessary. But even that skill only came with a little bit of Kara's tough love.

Remember my ugly break up with Ike? Well, that same day, after running out of his apartment, I wandered aimlessly around the North side of Chicago. I had no idea what to do or where to go after this man I thought I loved played paper shredder to my heart. The only place I could think of going was to Aunt Kara's. She and Benson, *whenever he wasn't on a drinking binge,* lived in Lincoln Park and a few stops south of Ike's apartment on the Brown Line train. I knew if I could get to her, everything would be alright. I thought that she would hold my hands, wipe my tears away and pray in every language possible for God to heal my brokenness. It didn't exactly go down like that.

I know I must have been a scary sight when I knocked on her door. The white lines of dried tears looked like a miniature version of the chalk outlines you see on television murder scenes. The mucus that dripped from my nose had been smeared across my cheek by my hand. My hair, recently braided, had lost any semblance of style and hung lifelessly on the side of my face.

"Jesus, CJ! What happened to you?"

Kara's eyes bulged when she saw me standing on her doorstep.

"Aunt Kara..." That was all the words I could muster at the moment.

Kara pulled me inside the house and spun me around. I guess she was checking for gun shot wounds or torn clothing. Yes, that's how bad I looked.

"Baby girl, what happened? Do I need to call the police?"

I shook my head. I found it ironic that I was in her house. Actually, I had not been to Aunt Kara's house in nearly five years. She always came over Nana's or met me and my Dad elsewhere. She probably didn't think anything of it, but for me, the memory of the last time I was there was still very vivid. I'd strategically avoided coming back and had been successful in doing so until now. Very funny, God.

"You have got to tell me something, Crystal."

So I told her everything. From the very beginning to how I ended up on her doorstep. Her facial expressions went back and forth from the motherly "everything is going to be alright, baby" gaze to the sistergirl "no, he didn't" neck roll several times before I got to the end of the story. Then, as I knew she would, she stood up and began pacing the floor. Her hips, grown wide by birthing two beautiful, wide-eyed babies, swayed as she thought about what I should do. For a moment, I had the fleeting image of what might have happened thirty years ago if this had been my mother telling her this awful situation. The way everyone talks about how bold my mother was, they probably would have called Aunt Toni and done something crazy, like put sugar in his tank. Pun very much intended. Then again, Aunt Kara has always been the reasonable one, so she probably would have turned the other cheek, as she has done with her husband for all of these years.

Anyway, I watched her pace for a while before I saw the familiar wringing of her hands. In spite of my heartache, I got a little bit excited. Like I said, Aunt Kara was a Pentecostal to her heart and when she started pacing and wringing her hands, I was sure demons and devils alike were shaking in their cloven boots. It meant she was about to pray and even better, I was going to be okay.

But that's not what happened at all that day. Aunt Kara got a word alright, especially after she saw the undeniable mixture of complete helplessness and total trust in my eyes. She stopped dead in her tracks and turned to me.

"Aren't you going to pray," I said.

"No." Her face still said she loved me, but her tone was as hard as stone.

I didn't know what to say. If Aunt Kara wouldn't pray for me, then I was doomed. Maybe this was karma. I was sitting in her house, having vowed never to return, asking her to pray for me. What audacity! She's right. She shouldn't pray for me. I didn't deserve her prayers.

Torn between a seething anger and the piercing stabs of guilt and shame, I stood up and began to walk towards the door.

Kara reached out and grabbed my arm before I could make my ill-informed getaway.

"I'm not going to pray because YOU are."

My eyes filled with the tears of both sadness and fear. This was not supposed to be a teachable moment, I thought. I needed something or someone to lean on and here she was telling me to stand by myself. Stand before God with all of this guilt and all of this shame and all of this hurt. I didn't know if I could do it.

"I will start, but you will finish this, CJ. Every woman gets hurt. This may have been the first time…"

If my head could have hung lower, I would have been kissing the floor. This certainly was not the first time.

"…and I'm sorry to say it won't be the last," she continued.

"God wants you to come to Him. I can't come to Him for you. I can only intercede so much. He wants you to trust Him and Him alone for your comfort."

I knew it was true. I had to learn for myself how to "battle in the spirit," as she says. Yet, even when I prayed that day with her, I didn't completely go there with God. There was still something I could not give Him. Although I know He already knows my heart, there was no way I was going to dare acknowledge the real source of my shame aloud. Definitely not in my prayers and definitely not there in that house.

74

***

A dark cloud is the only way I can describe this thing that's hung ominously over my head for most of my adolescence and all of my adulthood. It's almost as though I can see the light of God all around me, but can never fully step from under the darkness. Even the bright spots of my life are dim to me in comparison to the joy I've seen other people experience. I think this is probably the root of my never-ending cynicism and is most likely the reason I feel like I'm sometimes being held captive to the most unsavory, and definitely un-Christ-like thoughts.

I do have good days, though. Actually, most days are as good as I know good to be. I consider myself your average, run-of-the-mill, going-to-church-on-Sunday, praying-in-the-name-of-Jesus writer chick. I make my mistakes, I repent and I keep it moving. As long as I don't have to get too deep or surrender too much, I'm good. In other words, I have religion down pat. It's the whole "personal relationship" thing everyone talks about that I can't seem to grasp. I find myself remembering the small things people tell me God has forgotten. I can't imagine that He has, though. Forgotten, I mean.

My biggest challenge with my faith is reconciling the notion of unconditional love. The kind of love they (they being my Nana, Dad, Pastor and any other person I consider to be a spiritual authority figure) say God has for us. It's so hard to understand that because in my experience, everyone has conditions on their love. Even my father, who is the only one who comes closest to loving me that way, has conditions. If he didn't, then he probably would have remarried by now. It's like he has placed conditions on his love to my mother by saying he can only love her for the rest of his life. That no one else will have the privilege of knowing him the way she did because he has locked that part of his heart away forever. I know that might be a weird way of looking at it, but it's true. There will always be a part of my father I will never know simply because of the conditions he has placed on love and its function in his life.

And church folks are even worse. Half the time they cannot be trusted and in my experience, are the worse representatives of unconditional love. Their ability to love unconditionally is blocked by their own selective memory about how far they've come. How many people have been lost to the church because its members chose not to share their own struggles? Instead, they choose to point the finger at those who may not be fluent in the language of religion, but are seeking a place that will wrap them up in a love they cannot get in the world.

I can think of only one time in my life I may have purely identified and received love from both God and man with the fullness of my heart, mind and soul. I was five. FIVE! Even by the time I was eleven and skipped my little self down the aisle to accept Christ, I'd already been challenged by the notion of unconditional love. I'd seen how people have been hurt by it. So what do you think happened when I became a teenager? Of course by then, I'd seriously begun to doubt I would ever really be ready to give or receive it. Huh. No wonder my relationships never work out!

Another significant reason why I'm troubled by the idea of unconditional love is because I associate it with protection. To me, it's pretty simple. If God loves us in spite of us, then He will keep us from hurt and harm. Because I've known harm and even greater hurts, it is difficult to believe God's love is without condition. The fact I experience them, tells me my hurts have to be the result of some missed clause in the divine contract between me and God. On top of that, if the people who are supposed to love me, the ones that are right here on earth, can't protect me from harm, then how in the world do I count on God, who I cannot see, to do that?

Unconditional love? I'm sorry. There is just an uncertainty in it I don't think I can accept.

Maybe that's why I don't have many friends. Especially female friends. It's like there is this unwritten rule of loyalty among women I just don't buy. Something in me finds it hard to believe that at some point, a friend will not cross you. That your best girlfriend won't flirt with your man

76

or the co-worker you've gotten all chummy with at the after-work networking parties won't turn around and take your job. Even Deja, my college roommate, used to wonder how on a weekly basis, I could go from being the "coolest chick she knew" to something entirely different. She never gave me any reason to think she was not my friend, but I always imagined that one day she would. I know. Just call me cynical CJ. I'm working on that. But, I have to admit, it is very difficult. I've even tried to make friends with other women writers I've met at various conferences and online, but it still always seems like I'm waiting for the other shoe to drop and they can tell. One day, I'll be Ms. Chatterbox and the next, I can absolutely not bring myself to return a phone call. And that's not fair to them. The fact of the matter is, friends invest in each other and I don't know how to do that, unless I have a guaranteed return. Unfortunately, nothing in life is guaranteed.

The only exception in my life is Jonathan, but he's only an exception because he entered my life long before my issues did and therefore, by sheer length of association, has earned an exemption. Plus, he knows me and I can trust the me he knows is the real me, and not the manufactured me I've managed to put together over the years. Actually, he never let's me forget this either.

"I *know* you, CJ." Major emphasis on the word know, of course.

"You think you know me, Jon, but we aren't kids anymore. I've been through some things."

Even though I knew he was right, I couldn't possibly let him know that.

"Blah, blah, blah. What I do know is the pretty, little girl named Crystal Justine Germaine, who was carefree and mischievous and loved to play hopscotch and ride her big wheel, has grown up into a beautiful woman with big hair..." He reached out and touched my hair I was now wearing in a curly afro.

"What!"

"....AND who has mad issues!"

77

I have to admit, I was stuck for a moment on the fact he called me pretty and beautiful, until I realized he also said I had issues.

"Exactly. I have issues you have no clue about. Hence, you DON'T know me!"

His smile said otherwise. I felt my heart rate speed up. I hated to be wrong, but even worse, I hated when he was right.

"Please, girl. I know you have a big, ole' hole in your heart where a mother should be…"

"Wait a minute. You're going too far."

He continued.

"…I know you've spent much of your life writing about it instead of dealing with it.

"You don't know what you're talking about!"

And more.

"…I know your relationships with men suck because you won't allow yourself to receive good love from anyone except your dad, and you analyze everything and everyone to the nth degree."

My blood boiled, sending hot tears to my eyes and quivers through my body. That's when Jonathan grabbed my face. I tried to pull away from him, but he simply grabbed me again.

"But, I also know that the curious, sweet, lovely, little girl I met when I was six is still in there somewhere and she will always have me as her friend. Always."

I hated when he reads me like that. I hated it and I loved it. I only wished he did know everything.

***

The thing I cannot say. That's how I refer to my deepest secret. I think I do this because I know if I name it, then I'll bring life to it, and Lord knows, I want that part of my life to be dead and gone so bad I can taste it. So, I'm sitting in the place where joy should be is fear. Fear that my real story will be written for all to read. Fear that everything I know and love will be taken away from me as a result of it.

This fear has tried to take over me on more than one occasion. In fact, I can honestly say it feels like something hovering over me. The pits of my arms itch with it and every hair follicle on my body has been erected by the very thought of this thing I cannot say.

You are probably annoyed by me referring to it like that. Sorry.

I would love to be the type of person who could praise God in spite of trials and tribulations, but sometimes, I feel like I'd rather muddle through this thing angrily than to stand in the face of affliction and still have the strength to honor God. There is less guilt that way. The most courage I can gather at this point is to try to surrender this thing the best way I know how, and hope God sees the effort. In other words, enjoy the good days and deal with the bad days by not really dealing with them at all.

Surrendering is beyond a challenge for me because it requires me to let go of my complex about wanting to show people how good I am. Strange, huh? I guess I've always thought that if I could be good enough, then the secret that lie within my heart, the thing I cannot say, will go away and I won't have to worry about the damage it will do to all I hold dear.

I know what you're thinking. I do really wish I could just say it. Get it out. But, I know better than anybody that speaking something aloud can bring life to it, and if my secret was ever given life, I think it would be the death of me. In fact, I'm probably only alive because of the prayers of my father, grandmother and others that love me. My birth was symbolic of that fact. But, they won't be here forever and then what will I do?

Yeah, I'd have to be forced against my will to unveil the *thing I cannot say*. My will is pretty strong, so I doubt that would ever happen.

Part Two:
Implementation

Interlude

Natas was beyond glad. The first couple of hits had worked. The General was rather pleased, even though his pleasure seemed to only barely conceal his jealousy of the up-and-coming lieutenant. Nevertheless, the goal was still within reach and Natas seemed to have found the perfect strategy in stopping this seed from bearing fruit.

Many of the others in the demonic fleet had chosen a more direct approach to their tasks. They attacked in more obvious ways. They focused on stripping money and jobs and even the health from their subjects. That usually worked well for a season. However, Natas understood that even when they took away material things and threatened their physical well being, if they left a loving family structure in place, it would always be an uphill fight. More than that, if they failed to remove the subject's support system, especially one rooted in prayer and fasting, they would ultimately never gain victory against the Creator.

The only way to arrest a destiny; the only way to keep these worthless humans from being of any good use to the Enemy was to isolate them. Force them to see themselves only as the glorified dirt they are. Natas admittedly made some mistakes with Vivian and Sasha, but with this new generation, he was determined to not lose. The curse was firmly in place and working mightily on CJ.

Natas wouldn't stop now, especially if he wanted to unseat the General and become the newest lord of the earth. It was time to turn up the heat.

Chapter 9

CJ stood in front of the mahogany casket where the woman she called Nana rested in an eternal sleep.

"Too much makeup," she whispered in a voice that cracked with confusion and sorrow.

Her Nana was a natural beauty, she thought. But how natural is one in death? To CJ, there was nothing natural about the only woman in this world with blood the same as hers leaving her to navigate life alone. Nothing natural about that all.

It seemed like only yesterday CJ sat on the edge of her grandmother's bed with a heart heavy and broken with the thought of what was to come. The doctors had only given the old woman a few days to live.

"Why you sittin' up there crying, child? You better put a smile on your face right now."

It was just like Vivian to make it seem like nothing was wrong.

"Nana, you're acting like we are supposed to be happy that you're dying!"

CJ didn't want to sound harsh, but she had grown weary of people, even her Nana, telling her how she should feel.

The old woman looked at her grandchild. No, actually, she looked through CJ to her own child, Sasha, who would meet her shortly in the afterlife.

"No, baby, I just want you to be happy that in this moment, I'm still living."

The woman's eyes were still very much filled with the awareness that comes with 74 years of life. They were portals to her soul, revealing what her pride would not allow her to. Yet, even in her frailty, she was strong enough to know that all things, even good things, must come to an end. She was strong enough to know that the pains of this life are only significant, if there is no expectation of peace in the next. Unbeknownst to any of her family, she'd danced this slow dance with cancer for a while and although it had tried to twist and turn her, dip and shake her, she had now found her own rhythm and had taken the lead. She waited patiently for the next move, a word of release, and the freedom to finally stop dancing.

CJ smiled and decided to take full advantage of the last moments she had with her grandmother. They watched her favorite shows and listened to her favorite songs. Moments were the best way to describe the time they shared because the next morning, Vivian Grace Billingsley went home to be with the Lord.

***

CJ was in a really challenging place in her life. There was enough bad to wonder what in the world was happening and enough good for her to not want to end it all. Her career was taking off. She'd been promoted to senior editor at *Epic* and had decided to turn the millions of pieces of paper and hundreds of random scribbling in notebooks into a real book. A memoir.

In the midst of it all, she had this sense that so many of those she loved were leaving her in some way. Whether it was Nana dying, Jonathan going to New York for his new job or Aunt Toni finding out she had breast cancer, CJ had become all too acquainted with the weight of loss. The only separation that made any sense to her was Aunt Kara finally divorcing Uncle Benson. It was about time that happened.

If a person's funeral is a true indication of the impact they had while they lived, then Vivian was the Oprah of impact. Men and women alike stood at the microphone and shared stories of how one little ole' church lady on the south side of Chicago changed their lives. Whether it was showing kindness for the young mother who needed help raising her kids or the young man who learned the proper way to address a lady, the woman CJ called Nana had more "children" than anyone ever knew.

"Your grandmother sure was loved," Jonathan says to CJ as they are sitting on the couch at her grandmother's house eating the repast and receiving condolences.

CJ pretended she didn't hear him. Knowing this was tougher than she'd ever admit, Jonathan grabbed CJ's hand and held it.

Even while she chose to be mute that day, CJ's mind was extremely vocal.

I don't know how I feel about all of this. All of these people.

Did they really know my Nana?

What am I going to do without her?

Who am I going to turn to?

Finally, Jonathan, still holding her hand, stood up and nodded his head toward the door. CJ knew what this meant and followed him as he reached for his coat off of the wooden coat tree that stood in the foyer of the house. In that moment, a memory accosted her attention.

That coat tree has been in that same spot forever. When I was four, I took the word tree seriously and used to try to get my own coat by climbing it. My Nana would find me stuck half way up and crying because I couldn't go any further without it tipping over. At first, she'd chuckle at the sight of me. Then, she'd swat my bottom and swiftly gather me and my coat from the tree.

It's funny how loss offers clarity in some ways and complete ambiguity in others.

CJ turned towards Jonathan who was watching her from the door. The emotions on his face were pure and genuine. He was torn. On the one hand, he wanted to stay and comfort his friend, knowing this was probably one of the worse days of her life. On the other hand, he had exactly two hours to catch his plane back to New York where his six-month-old job and one-year-old relationship waited for him to continue the new life he'd built there after leaving Chicago and the death of his own mother.

CJ just stared at him. Her coal-black eyes looking like the kindergartener he'd met for the first time so many years ago. Encased around the almond-shaped pools of sorrow were eyelashes that barely curled as they tried desperately to hold on to her tears. Jonathan knew CJ's pain because it was his own and yet he was also very uncomfortable with what he felt rising up from the depths of his soul as he stood there looking at the girl he's known forever.

"I have to go," he said.

"I know."

"Everything is going to be alright."

She wanted to say she knew that too, but she didn't.

"Okay."

Jonathan walked over and hugged her. She held him a little longer than appropriate, although on that day it didn't matter to anyone, especially her. She wanted to tell him to stay. To pray with her. To help her understand why cancer chose her Nana and not someone else's. But, she didn't think it was right. It wasn't right to wish cancer on someone else, no matter who it would save. And it wasn't right to keep her friend here just because she was hurting. Plus, if he wanted to stay, he would.

Jonathan finally stepped back from CJ's embrace. He kissed her on the forehead and left. CJ remained standing at the door for a full fifteen minutes before someone noticed, told her father and Langston took his daughter upstairs to lie down and rest.

***

The divorce between Benson and Kara was only slightly less than ugly. Langston knew his friend struggled with a number of vices, but had thought that after almost thirty years, he'd pulled himself together and returned to being the God-fearing man he'd known most of his life. Kara had obviously hoped the same thing, as she stayed with him in spite of his bouts with alcohol and occasional wandering. That was, until this last episode. Having cried her last tear,

85

Kara finally filed for divorce after being embarrassed in the one place she'd found solace.

Kara was a trustee at Mt. Moriah Baptist Church. After completing his last stint in rehab, Benson had been restored as a deacon. Held in high esteem, the couple had met and married at the church and both of their children, now grown, were raised in the church's many youth programs. While church folk and outsiders may have gossiped behind closed doors about where they'd last seen Deacon Benson or who with, their outside chatter seemed to never overpower the respect many had for Kara, her service to the church and to God.

It had been a couple of months since Benson returned from rehab and shared his testimony at the church. In the midst of all the "Praise the Lords" and "He's a delivers," Kara couldn't help but to feel like something was still not right. Yes, he was coming home every night and participating in all of the church activities. Yes, he smiled at the right time and to the right people but, to her, it was all a farce. When they went home, there was a wall the size of the Sears tower between them. He'd sit in the living room on the computer or watching TV and she, well, she'd sit in the living room watching him. As she had done so many times before, Kara prayed that God would heal their marriage. This time, however, she had no peace in her heart He would.

After helping Langston and CJ with the repast for Ms. Vivian's funeral, Kara returned home to find Benson sitting on the edge of the sofa with his head in his hands, sobbing uncontrollably. It was a Saturday night, so she was shocked to even find him home, much less in the condition he was in. Thinking that maybe she'd walked in on a breakthrough, Kara quickly sat down next to her husband, rubbed his back and began to pray. Just as the prayer began to intensify, Benson jumped up suddenly, turned to Kara as though he was going to say something, then deciding against it, went into their bedroom and slammed the door. Her prayers intercepted, Kara felt a heaviness settle into her soul as she simply got up and began preparing Sunday dinner.

That Sunday morning, Kara called CJ as she'd done every week to see if she was actually coming to church instead of watching the service streaming online. She could never understand how these young people with their tiny phones and computers could get the same experience watching the pastor preach on those itty-bitty screens that she did right there in person. Nevertheless, they were getting the Word and that really was all that mattered. Surprisingly, CJ said she was coming to church that morning. Kara knew CJ was taking her grandmother's death hard and was grateful the young woman was seeking comfort in the church. However, she had to admit she was also excited about CJ being there for other reasons. Somewhere deep down she had a feeling she was going to need some back up.

Kara always arrived at church before anyone else, including the Pastor. The main reason was because she held keys and could open the building, turn on the heat or air conditioning and get everything ready for the day of worship. The other reason was because she felt a sense of peace in the quiet of the sanctuary. It was almost as if the building was one large lap she could crawl onto and share her heart with her Father. She often would kneel down at the altar and, instead of praying the fiery, "shake the gates of hell" prayers she was known for, she could pray and meditate with a whisper; finding rest in the words of the Almighty she could only hear in the silence and solitude.

At least in that sense, this day was no different.

After praying her heart and soaking the altar with her tears, Kara heard the familiar, still Voice.

Whatever you do, hold your peace.

It sounded more like a warning than direction. Either way, Kara would be obedient.

Several of the ushers walked into the sanctuary just as Kara finished praying. Standing to her feet, she plastered her Sunday-morning smile onto her face and spoke to the women.

"Praise the Lord, ladies."

They did not respond.

She didn't find it odd the women did not bother to speak to her. Many people found it hard to get started in the morning. She placed her Bible and jacket at the end of the second row, as she did every week, and headed to the restroom. More people walked into the sanctuary.

"Hi, Sis. Johnson. How's that grandbaby of yours?"

Sis. Johnson looked at Kara with her mouth twisted into a frown.

"Fine. Just fine." She said rather tersely.

Kara wasn't moved by her attitude. Sis. Johnson never really cared for her, anyway.

It wasn't until Kara realized everyone she spoke to either ignored her or responded with short, one-word answers it dawned on her that something was up. That's when she ran into CJ who was coming out of one of the classrooms holding what looked like a white flyer. The same one that everyone else was holding.

"Aunt Kara, I'm so sorry!"

"Hey, babygirl! What 'chu sorry for?"

"Oh, Aunt Kara!"

Realizing she didn't know anything, CJ pulled Kara into the old choir room.

"You don't know?"

"Know what?" But even then, Kara's stomach sank.

CJ handed Kara the flyer/letter.

"A young lady was passing these out in front of the church."

Dear Members of Mt. Moriah Baptist Church,

Please forgive me for interrupting your worship service. However, I can no longer hold in my heart how I feel and I think it is important for you to know what kind of people you have in your church. Even as I write this, I know what I'm doing will hurt a lot of people, but my hope is that you will place yourself in my shoes.

I was raised in the church. I know that Deacons are supposed to be looked upon as great men of God. The Bible says they are supposed to be faithful to their wives and stay away from strong drink. Well, I'm sorry to say that one among you has not been keeping that vow very well. I know that everyone knows that Deacon Williams, also known as Benson, has had a drinking problem in the past. Unfortunately, that is not all he has.

For the last year, I've been having an affair with Deacon Williams.(If anyone doubts I am telling the truth, I can share with you some intimate details that will, without a doubt, prove what I'm saying is true.) This was not a one-time thing. I believe we are in love. I am not proud of my relationship with him because I know it is adultery, but, as I have said, I'm at the point where I have no other options. Anyway, yesterday I told Benson I was pregnant with his child and at first, I thought he would be happy. We went to my house, made love, and then, he began to drink. A lot. I'll admit, this scared me a bit because he'd stopped drinking over the last couple of months. But then, everything turned bad. He began to hit me. For an hour, he went back and forth between telling me how much he loved me (which I still believe) to smacking me around. I tried to leave so he could calm down, but he wouldn't let me. Finally, he left. I've tried to call him. I've tried to reach him, but he won't return my calls. I know he may just be scared, but after waiting all night for him to call me, I began to panic.

I am eighteen years old. I have no family. I have no money. I don't know why I'm writing this letter except to say this man is all I have. I know he and his wife are "pillars" of this church, but I will do anything I have to do to either bring him back to me or make sure he pays for what he's done to me.

I'm so sorry.
MOJ

After reading the letter, Kara's limbs felt heavy. Her face burned hot with anger and embarrassment, and her eyes were completely blurred by her tears. Before she could find a verbal response to the pain, everything went black. Kara passed out in CJ's arms.

CJ was beside herself with both rage and sadness. One sentence stood out to her from all the other horrible ones. *I am eighteen years old.* She was so tempted, even if it was selfish, to unload her own pain right then and there. And yet, holding the woman who served as a mother to her after losing her own, and after losing the grandmother who was her everything, she knew she could never release her own pain without deepening Kara's and ultimately, losing her, too.

After coming to, Kara stood up quickly and marched back into the church sanctuary. Like the final hit of the ninth inning of a tied baseball game, a hush fell over the church as they watched one of their beautiful mothers walk slowly and carefully down the aisle. Everyone was anticipating an explosion. Those that had already cast judgment were even prepared for her defense. What they got, however, was a typical, if strangely solemn, Sunday service. The Pastor preached a sermon on the importance of praying for those who are hurting and everyone, including Kara, pretended to listen.

In fact, the only thing she heard for the rest of that day was the familiar, still Voice from earlier.

Whatever you do, hold your peace.

When she returned home, Benson's things were gone. The next day, she visited an attorney.

***

"Dad, why are you trying to run interference between Kara and Benson?"

"Because they are both my friends."

Langston hated arguing with his daughter, but CJ had become very aggressive lately when it came to how she felt about the whole situation between Kara and Benson.

"You need to get some new friends," CJ muttered under her breath.

"I heard that."

Feeling bold and completely out of sorts after the events of the last month, CJ decided to confront her father.

"Good. I'm glad you heard me. You do recall what Benson did to Kara, right?"

90

Langston knew alright. He was completely stunned. He'd just talked to his boy a week prior to the incident and it seemed like everything was going pretty well. He'd reconciled with Kara...again. Benson even had told him he'd prayed to God and had finally put his drinking and womanizing away forever in order to work on rebuilding his marriage. Then, what seemed like out of nowhere, everything falls apart. He hated to say it, but he didn't know who Benson was anymore. What happened to the good brother who loved the Lord and adored his wife? The old Benson would have never lied to Langston like that. Something had happened to him and it seemed like the prayers of everyone who ever loved him never reached the ears of God.

"Yes, CJ. I do know what he did. It was horrible, but..."

"But!? But!? How can there be a *but*?

There was no way CJ was ever going to understand the bond Langston shared with both Benson and Kara. They were his link to Sasha. Without them, Sasha probably would have never been his wife and when she died, they were the ones that helped him manage those first few years raising CJ without the woman he loved so dearly. Langston was connected to these two people and he prayed for their reconciliation daily, even in the face of such a horrible breach.

"You will never understand what both Kara and Benson mean to me."

Oh, but CJ knew. She could feel the memory of Sasha bearing down on her as her father continued to talk.

"They are both special people and I remember when their love was real; when everything was good and blessed. I'm hoping they can get there again."

He can't be serious, CJ thought.

Langston was very serious. So much so that he planned to invite both of them to his upcoming retirement party.

Chapter 10

Standing near the baggage claim of Alpha Airlines in O'Hare International Airport, CJ's nerves were frayed. It had been three months since Nana died and the whole thing with Benson and Kara exploded in front of everyone who mattered. And yet, the passing of time could not stop her from feeling she was hovering only barely above the grasp of the deepest and darkest depression ever. Even her work at the magazine, the interviews with celebrities and other famous folk, could not excite her enough to yank her out of the blahs. For her, the only person who could even remotely do that was sitting in a plane on the tarmac just outside of the building where she stood.

Equally nervous, Jonathan sat in his seat waiting for the okay to exit the plane where he'd spent the last two-and-a-half hours watching two pretty flight attendants battle for his attention. In another time in his life, it would have been fun to play one woman, a short, curvy beautiful brown island girl against the other, a tall, model-esque sister with full lips and skin the color of extra-sweet coffee. He never thought he'd ever hear him say it, but he'd had his fill of all of that. More than anything right now, he desired the familiar. Even as he struggled with how to look sophisticated in spite of the proverbial tail between his legs, Jonathan knew that coming home was the best thing he could do right now.

In his phone call to CJ two weeks earlier, he'd cryptically announced that New York was not for him. CJ knew better, though. Jonathan was not a runner. He didn't just up and leave any place without good cause. Something major had happened and she would get to the bottom of it because she knew he could never keep anything from her anyway. Plus, pressing him for the details was going to be even easier, since she agreed to let him crash at her apartment until he could get back on his feet again.

Fifteen minutes later, CJ saw the familiar swagger and canyon dimples of her best friend. She always seemed to forget how attractive Jonathan was until she sees him after a long absence.

Of course, knowing he used to eat boogers when we were kids probably doesn't help much.

But, as he walked toward the moving belt searching for his luggage and not yet noticing her, she was reminded of just how much the little brown boy had grown up and determined to shake away the not-so innocent thoughts that popped into her head.

"Hey, you." CJ tapped him on the shoulder.

Turning around quickly, Jonathan responded, "Hey, yourself."

The two made their way to the car in relative silence. Both wanted to share the personal trials they'd endured over the last few months, but neither wanted to interfere with the other's thoughts. Too polite to admit it, they needed each other and although they both wanted to leave the floor open for the other to unload their burdens, they were also too consumed by their own turmoil to have the energy to process it. CJ was the first to break the silence as they exited the airport and made their way down I-94.

"You know, they say the manner in which you were born will determine the tone of your life."

Jonathan knew where this was going. They'd had this conversation a million times before and with everything that was going on with him, he didn't really want to have it again.

"Not necessarily," he said, trying to not sound disinterested.

"It's true!"

It wasn't true. At least that is what he hoped. Because if it was, then it would mean he would become the man his father was, something he'd tried to avoid his whole life. Maybe if he just entertained her a bit, then he could get on with what was really bothering him.

"Okay, I'll play your little game. So what existential truth about your life did you derive this time?"

CJ paused. She knew he was sick of her trying to make sense of her life, but as much as she loved writing about other people, it was her own life she was most curious about. Especially now that everyone she's ever depended on seemed to be pulling, or being pulled, away.

"Well, I think that since I took my mother's life upon entering the world, I will spend the rest of my time on earth giving life."

Jonathan stared back at CJ with the most confused look she'd ever seen on his face. Then, just as suddenly, he broke out in a loud, obnoxious laughter.

Between breaths he said, "So when is the baby due!"

CJ didn't take too well to being made fun of so she thumped him on the arm, nearly swerving out of her lane.

"Hey! Don't kill us, Socrates!"

"Stop it, Jon, I'm serious!"

"So am I." He continued to cackle like a baritone chicken.

Finally, he said, "Come on, woman. You must be reading those self-help books again. I can always tell because when you do, you always seem to come up with these twisted mission statements for your life; stuff that makes no sense to me whatsoever. What's wrong with just living? Why do you constantly make your mother's death about you?"

"Because it *is* about me!"

Perturbed, CJ decided to hit below the belt.

"Why do I even talk to you? You don't know how it feels. You *had* your mother, didn't you?"

Jonathan grew silent. CJ was like a sister to him, but she'd hit a painful nerve. Yes, he'd had his mother and just like CJ, he'd lost her. He couldn't believe how insensitive CJ had become in the time he'd been away.

CJ knew she was wrong. She knew how much Jonathan loved his mother and how her death had injured him greatly. He'd just gotten back in town and she'd already begun her attack. She found herself on the defensive quite a bit lately. Apologetically, she lowered her voice.

"Aw, Jonny. I'm so sorry. That did not come out the way I intended. Everything has just been so crazy lately."

Jonathan kept his head down. He heard her, but his mind was still a million miles away or at least 1,000 or so. CJ pulled the car into a parking space in front of her apartment building. After turning the car off, she turned to look at Jonathan.

"I just thought if I could understand the connection between me and her, then maybe I can differentiate myself enough where people will stop comparing me to her. Maybe then, I could live my life the way it was meant to be lived."

Jonathan looked at CJ with deep sadness etched across his face. She'd never seen him look that way and even then, because she was consumed by her own issues, ranting about her own needs, she nearly missed it. Words sat on Jonathan's tongue anxious for freedom and yet he knew that once he said them, he would have to acknowledge and accept his own failure. He didn't know if he was ready to do that yet. So he chose to respond differently.

"I understand, Cris."

CJ quickly noticed his use of the long-abandoned nickname he called her when they were in elementary school. It was like an alarm waking her out of her selfish trance and allowing her to focus her natural and spiritual eyes on her friend. She finally saw his pain and realized how much he needed her.

"Jon?"

95

"Yes."

"What's wrong?"

His response was as random as it was clear.

"It was a woman."

***

Jonathan had spent much of his life struggling against the model of manhood presented to him by his father. The elder Cooper left him and his mother when he was four years old; barely bothering to check back in with his boy and never once taking the time to show him what it really meant to be a man. Everything Jon learned, from how to tie a tie to how to ask a girl out on a date, he learned from the women in his life or from television. These "lessons" taught Jonathan early on how to please women, even if it meant also learning how to manipulate them to get what he wanted.

Even more than his own areas of lack, Jonathan hated what his father's departure did to his mother. As a young boy growing up, he remembered hearing his mother crying and praying in her bedroom located in the very back of their townhouse. He used to think her sorrow was because of some problem she was having at work or some fight she was having with his grandmother who, in her overbearing way, would often give unasked for, and sometimes unwarranted, advice. As the years went on, he figured out some of those tears were the result of her loneliness and the anxiety that being both mother and father to a young boy, and trying your best to do both well, brought.

Both old and young women loved Jonathan. Or at the very least, were infatuated with him. As a child, the gray-haired mothers from church would pinch his cheeks and comment on how handsome he was, and how his mother needed to invest in bats in order to keep the "fast" girls away from him.

He took all of this in and decided he didn't need a father or father figure to get the attention or nurturing he so desperately craved. Everything he could ever want, he could find in a woman. Unfortunately, in each relationship, he'd drain the woman he was with and then, having learned all

96

that he could, after getting his fill, he'd move on to the next one. He was eager to explore the newness of relationship again and again, but unknowingly held on to the one thing his father gave him: A lack of commitment. Evidence of this was in the fact that no one could ever pin a "type" on him. He dated the spectrum of women: tall, short, thin, thick, dark, light, smart, not-so-smart, wealthy, poor, educated and uneducated. Each one taught him something, but none of them could ever hold his attention. Well, that's not entirely true. One woman held his heart for what seemed like a lifetime and another one, just long enough to break it.

"What do you mean it was a woman?"

CJ and Jonathan had made it into the house after sitting silently in the car for ten minutes. She had no idea what his random statement meant, but didn't want to rush him into explaining either.

Jonathan took a sip from the glass of lemonade CJ handed him.

"I left Chicago because of a woman and I've returned because of one."

CJ had to admit she wasn't surprised. Jonathan always had his share of women. She remembered when they were growing up and every so often the pastor of their church would issue an altar call for those who wanted to pray for God's forgiveness for "unrighteous" acts. CJ would always get poked by her dad because she couldn't hold back her laughter as she watched Jon practically run to the altar with tears streaming down his face. He was sincere about wanting to change, but it always seemed like a force much greater than himself kept him running in and out of the arms of women.

This time seemed different though. In his eyes, she didn't just see the standard remorse for hurting someone. The sorrow was deeper, almost like it was etched in his chestnut-brown eyes like stone. And behind the sorrow was exhaustion and resignation.

"I didn't know you were dating someone when you left here?"

"Nobody did. I don't think I even really knew."

CJ let him talk it out.

"I met her at a conference I went to at McCormick Place. She was gorgeous. One of the most beautiful women I'd ever seen."

CJ ignored the prick she felt.

"..and?"

"And we spent the entire conference together. When she flew back to New York, she asked me to come back with her and I said no."

"If you liked Ms. Beautiful so much, why didn't you go?"

"Because I know my track record. It was too soon after Mom died and I really didn't think it was going to go any further."

"But it did."

"It did. Jordyn...that's her name...Jordyn and I talked on the phone every single night and for the first time, I didn't feel like I was milking someone. I didn't feel like a student trying to play some twisted life catch-up game. We shared equally with each other. Kind of like me and you. It was then that I knew it wasn't just a fling."

"Sounds like the start of a great friendship."

Jonathan just looked at CJ. That was such a loaded statement.

"It was definitely more than friendship."

"Okay. So, I still don't understand what went wrong."

Jonathan didn't either, but tried to explain it the best he could.

"Well, after six months of talking and flying back and forth to see each other, we discussed being together. She told me her cousin owned a marketing firm in Manhattan and that she could probably get me a job there. She also had a girlfriend who would give me a break on the deposit for an apartment in Harlem."

"So you moved."

"I moved." Jonathan sat in silence for a full five minutes.

CJ was so tired of pulling teeth, but knew whatever happened to him in the Big Apple had to have been serious, so she remained attentive. He finally continued.

"As you know, I moved out there a little over six months before Ms. Vivian passed..."

He paused, unsure if the mention of her grandmother's name would affect CJ. She smiled and encouraged him to continue.

"I'd decided I was going to turn over a new leaf. New city, new woman, new me, you know?"

CJ wished she did. She looked down at her watch before commenting on his attempt at a renaissance.

"Well, for the two hours you've been back, you definitely seem different. I'm just trying to figure out if that's a good thing or not."

"It was, at first. I did everything for Jordyn. I put my heart out there as much as I knew how to, but it was never enough."

"What do you mean it was never enough?"

Jonathan was stuck. How could he explain it?

"For the first time in my life, I'd committed to a woman. I prayed God would show me what to do and He did. That's big, CJ."

Yeah, that was big. He was seeking God for direction and not man...or in this case, woman.

"After about a month or so of my being there, everything seemed to change."

"Changed?"

"Yeah. She kept saying I wasn't fully there with her. That my heart and mind was somewhere else. She said something wasn't connecting between us."

He paused as confusion shadowed his face.

"I had no idea what she was talking about!"

"Was it?"

"Was what?"

"Was your heart and mind somewhere else?"

Jonathan didn't answer her and CJ didn't press him.

99

"I still don't understand, Jon. Even if she thought you guys weren't connecting, that still doesn't explain why you moved so quickly back to Chicago."

Jonathan kept telling himself to *man up* before sharing this part of the story. He was tired of his emotions pulling at him and he didn't want to appear weak, even in front of his best friend.

The pain he felt in telling the next part of the story was evident to CJ. She was familiar with his look of sadness and moved from the papasan chair where she sat cross-legged to the couch next to him.

"After I returned to New York from your grandmother's funeral, I thought Jordyn was going to pick me up from the airport. However, when I got off the plane, I got a text from her saying she had to work late and would see me later."

Each word became more labored as Jonathan's tone dropped a register and he tried to maintain some control.

"My dumb self, instead of going home and getting some much-needed rest, decides to surprise her at her office."

Jonathan couldn't bring himself to say anymore.

"She was there?"

"Yes, she was there."

"With someone else?"

"Yes."

CJ knew Jonathan wasn't just torn up about being cheated on, even though she imagined it must have hurt to see the woman he'd moved halfway across the country for with another man. But Jonathan was more upset with himself. He'd finally decided to trust his heart to someone, only to have the one he gave it to disregard him and his efforts.

He was also mad at God. Mad that he took a chance and trusted God to direct his path when it came to his relationships with women, only to find out the path led him straight to heartache.

"I know this must be hard, Jon, and I don't mean to make it worse. But, I have to say, in this entire time you've been telling me this story, I never heard you once say you loved her."

Jonathan burned with anger. Jordyn had said the same thing the last time they argued before he left New York.

"Did you love her?"

He didn't know. He honestly didn't know. He'd only loved one woman and that, he thought, was something totally different.

CJ took his silence to mean no. She was surprised at the relief that swept over her.

Jonathan thought maybe this was his past coming back to haunt him. Or maybe he did have some unresolved issues that kept him from connecting with Jordyn and loving her the way she needed to be loved. Maybe he, with all of his trying and doing, was still too emotionally immature. Maybe he pushed her into the arms of another man.

It never occurred to him that maybe he'd just committed to the wrong woman and that the right one was the one he'd loved with certainty since he was six.

Chapter 11

The following month felt like first-grade all over again for CJ and Jonathan. Every night was filled with laughter as they spent time watching their favorite television shows and talking until the wee hours of the morning. In a way, they renewed each other and, in spite of the craziness that lingered around them, they both felt a normalcy they hadn't in a long time.

With Jonathan around, CJ felt safe. Not just physically, but emotionally and even spiritually. They'd started praying together after dinner and wrapped in the security that Jon's presence provided her, CJ began to explore her hidden thoughts, opening her heart to the possibility of being free of the pain of the past. In fact, journaling became an important part of her day and as the weeks went by, she found herself digging deeper and understanding more.

"Hey, CJ, can I use your laptop? Mine is being worked on and I want to check my email to see if there have been any responses to the resumes I sent out this week."

The writer in CJ was leery of giving anyone her laptop. Even her best friend. It was like handing over her children to a complete stranger. Jonathan, however, was not a stranger, and with that thought, she reached into her bag and handed him her laptop. In essence, she also handed him essentially every thought that had crossed her mind and found its way to her pen over the last year. She then headed out the door to meet her dad to discuss his upcoming retirement party.

After twenty minutes or so of attempting to watch television, Jonathan finally sat down at the wooden desk that filled a quarter of the small living room and turned on the laptop. A document that CJ had been working on earlier popped up on the screen. She must have just put her computer on sleep and planned to come back to it later, Jonathan said to himself. Before he could click save, he was drawn to the words that seemed to leap out of the screen to him.

My experience with boys might have been limited as a teenager, but my experience with men was certainly not.

Jonathan turned away quickly as he felt his stomach twist in knots. A part of him wanted to continue reading, to finally know what kept CJ so distant, even when she pretended not to be. Another part of him knew if he read her private thoughts, he would not only be crossing a line in their friendship ensuring its demise, but that everything, including how he felt about her deep down in that place he'd been careful to hide, would change. He'd have to love her aloud and in the open. And if he continued reading, he was also going to have to sacrifice his friendship in order to alleviate the burden CJ had carried for so long.

I was young. Fifteen years old. I didn't know how to say no. I didn't know that I could say no.

Curiosity and a genuine desire to help his friend end whatever pain she held in her heart all these years took over. Instead of closing the document, Jonathan read every detail. The little girl he'd met so long ago loomed large from the page.

I couldn't have known. Or maybe I did and just didn't know what to do about it. I know I'm not supposed to say that it is my fault, but it's hard not to think that. I'd babysat for them a thousand times and nothing like that had ever happened before that day. But of course, he was never there.

The kids were asleep and I was lying across the bed watching my favorite syndicated television show in their guest room. To this day, I can't bring myself to watch "Business Women." Anyway, I was lying across the bed when he came in. I could smell the alcohol from 10 feet away, but that wasn't unusual. There was always something weird and broken about him, but I always figured most grown people had something weird and broken going on with them. Some you could see better than others.

He asked me if the kids were asleep. They were. Smiling, he sat on the edge of the bed. I heard the little Voice then. It told me to leave. It told me to go home. But dad hated for me to take the train late at night and they did said it was okay for me to sleep over when I sat for them. I should have left.

At first, it was just regular talk. Chit Chat. How was school? Did I get good grades? I answered those questions well enough. He told me he appreciated me helping them out. He even said God would bless me for it.

The bile that had begun to form at the base of Jon's throat inched its way up. He'd used many an insincere line before, but never could he see himself using God as a means to... Jonathan fearfully anticipated what was coming next.

I kept wondering why he was making a big deal out of it. I mean, they were paying me. At that point, I just wanted to go to sleep. I thought maybe if I stretched and yawned he'd get the message. He got a message alright. Just not the one I was trying to give him. He asked me if I was tired and I said yes. Bad move.

He asked if I wanted a massage. He said massages were good tension relievers, especially after running behind two grade-school kids all day. I never remember answering him. I can't remember saying, "Yes, I want a massage." The next thing I remember is laying on my stomach as his hands rubbed my back.

The most confusing part of all of this, the thing that hurts me the most, is not that I let him massage me, but that, if I'm honest, it felt good. I'm ashamed of that. I really am.

In my dreams, everything stops with the massage. Something intervenes in that moment. Sometimes it's keys in the door signaling the arrival of his wife. Sometimes it's the phone that rings and stops him in his tracks. Unfortunately, that's only in my dreams. That night, the massage was only the beginning. I still smell the stench of alcohol, sweat and tears whenever I see him. Maybe that's why dad is always asking me why I turn my nose up when that man walks into the room. Of course, he doesn't know it's not intentional. I just can't help it. I smell that awful day every time that man is around and it's a reminder of how everything changed for me. That day, I changed. Innocence, in any form, was not only stolen, but has eluded me ever since.

Even as he read, his heart broke. Jon could not believe in all these years, CJ did not trust him enough to share this with him. While he understood the violation she experienced at the hands of someone who was supposed to protect her, who was supposed to be a great friend to her family, could make her shut down, he also remembered how much they'd already shared with each other. Burdens had found relief in the bosom of their friendship. It was hard to understand why this was any different. Nevertheless, Jonathan was familiar with how secrets can consume you. There was a time when his own skeletons closed him off to anything real.

A gasp, sharp and painful, resounded loudly in the room. Jonathan was so consumed by anger and sorrow that he hadn't heard CJ come in. Until then. When he turned around and looked at her, it seemed as if he was staring at a ghost. A few short hours ago, her face was full and she seemed rather happy. They both did. Now, looking past him to the screen that held the words that were almost sacred to her, her cheeks

105

seemed gaunt and her eyes bulged with shock. Following the loud gasp of air she took in when she saw the hardest parts of her life laid bare, she sighed in a way that sounded like she was deflating. Like her breath was being squeezed out through the growing hole in her soul.

"Cris..." Jonathan helplessly watched betrayal shadow his friend's face.

CJ's only words were a whisper. "How could you?"

***

She'd always believed the concept of friendship was a mediocre one at best and that someday everyone, no matter who they were, would end up disappointing her. However, CJ always thought her history with Jonathan made him exempt from that. She never thought she would have to question the loyalty of the only friend she trusted. And yet, here she was looking at a man who'd not only invaded her privacy, but had tried to rationalize it. His betrayal and the subsequent heartache that followed sent her storming furiously out of her apartment and driving aimlessly throughout the city. As she sped down Lake Shore Drive, she thought about where she could go or to whom she should turn. There was no one. Anyone she would have normally ran to for consolation, would eventually want to know what was so private she could not share it with her best friend. She sped faster down the winding road as it turned from Lake Shore to South Shore Drive. As fast as she was moving, you would have thought she was being chased. And I guess in a way, she was. Her pursuer, a mountain of a secret, was rapidly catching up with her.

After driving for 45 minutes, CJ ended up in Hammond, Indiana. She pulled into the parking lot of one of five hair salons owned by her godmother, Cassandra. Ms. Cassie had moved to Indiana about fifteen years prior and although Hammond was a short drive from the South Side of Chicago, CJ didn't make it out there as often as she should. Actually, she hadn't visited in a couple of years and didn't know if Ms. Cassie would even be there. As she pushed open the glass door, CJ heard the voice before she saw the face.

"Thank you, Jesus!"

CJ wasn't too happy with God right then, so hearing Ms. Cassie's exclamation of praise almost sent her walking back out the door. But she didn't go. She breathed in the pungent scent of hair relaxer, stepped into the salon and into the arms of her godmother.

"I promise I was just thinking about you!"

"Hi, Ms. Cassie."

"Look at you." Ms. Cassie held CJ's hand and gave her a ballerina twirl in order to get the full view of the young woman. CJ felt like a teenager, half-embarrassed and half-pleased about the attention.

"If I could have that figure back...child, please!"

Everyone in the salon laughed at Ms. Cassie's implication, knowing full well the old woman loved to talk about getting her "brick house" figure back even though at 60 and a very-fit size 12, most people would say she'd never lost it.

Ms. Cassie led CJ to the back office where they both sat down on the eclectic orange couch that served as extra seating.

"So what brings you by to see Ms. Cassie, baby?"

CJ started to apologize for not stopping by sooner, but Cassie quickly raised her hand to stop her from speaking.

"And I don't want to hear no apologies about why you ain't been by here, either. You are a busy young lady writing for that big-time magazine. I'm proud of you. Now, let's get to the meat of it. What's going on?"

CJ smiled gratefully at Cassie and proceeded to tell her the whole story. Well, not the whole story, but enough so she could get the picture. She was grateful Ms. Cassie didn't ask for any more details than she gave.

"You have a man living with you?"

CJ knew this would be the first hurdle she'd have to jump. Ms. Cassie, although she was truly a precious and understanding woman, was still a believer in the Bible and Jonathan living with CJ, even if temporarily, was not going to sit well with her.

107

"It's little Jonny! You remember him. He lived next door to me and Dad when I was growing up."

Ms. Cassie didn't respond.

"We're just friends, Ms. Cassie. He just moved back home from New York after a bad break up. He's looking for a new job and apartment and..."

Cassie waved her hand as if to say that no more explanation was needed or wanted. CJ continued.

"...he's going to be moving out soon. Especially now."

Cassie's eyes spoke wisdom even before her mouth confirmed it.

"For someone you call *just a friend*, someone you are supposedly angry with for betraying your trust, you sure seem to have worked up enough explanations to plead in his case."

CJ gave up. The last thing she wanted was to get hung up on this one detail, but a part of her felt like she had to justify her actions, and yes, maybe defend Jonathan a little bit.

Cassie was not moved by CJ's silence. She'd been here before.

"Are you really angry at your friend or are you more angry he discovered this secret of yours?"

It was CJ's turn to not respond.

Cassie chuckled. She was amused by her goddaughter's stubbornness, knowing she got it honestly.

"Baby, secrets are heavy. I know that better than anybody. You try to carry them too long by yourself and you'll find yourself broken. Have you ever thought that maybe God has allowed this to happen for a reason? That maybe it is time for you to stop carrying this by yourself?"

CJ had to admit a part of her was relieved someone else knew. She still hated the way Jonathan found out, but she also knew it was inevitable someone was going to find out that way. Fear kept her so bound that if she was ever going to be free, it was going to take every angel in heaven to get her to the point where she could reveal it. And having Jonathan there by her side when she did was actually not so bad.

CJ smiled at her godmother, thinking it could only have been God that led her to the woman.

Cassie watched CJ work over every detail of what she'd just said in her head. It amazed her how after thirty years, some things never changed.

Cassie reached out to touch CJ's hand and said, "I've had this conversation before, you know."

CJ stood up quickly and picked up her purse. For her, their little advice session was taking an all-too familiar turn.

"I'm going to get out of here, Ms. Cassie. Thank you so much for listening and…for sharing."

Ms. Cassie stood up and hugged CJ. Holding her tightly in her arms, she whispered in her ear.

"You are so much like her, baby. More than you'll ever know. And that's *not* a bad thing."

CJ's eyes welled with tears. Every emotion she could fathom burst forth as she sobbed against the full bosom of her godmother. While it hurt her to do it, in those ten minutes they stood embracing, she allowed the pain to pour out. She missed her grandmother. She missed her best friend, the six-year-old she'd met all those years ago and who saw in her the beauty and grace she never did. She missed the childhood she'd never known. The one with a father who didn't live in perpetual grief and was always there to protect her. And yes, she missed her mother.

CJ wiped her face and pulled back from Ms. Cassie whose smile made her warm on the inside. She'd been confronted by Sasha again and this time, she'd allowed herself to feel everything that came with that.

Yet, in spite of the mini-breakthrough, CJ still didn't know if she was very comfortable with being "like" her mother. She had no idea what that meant. But she did know she needed to get back home to her friend.

***

CJ opened the door to her small apartment very slowly. It was late when she finally made it back to the city and she wasn't sure if Jonathan would be asleep. She actually hoped he wouldn't be because she desperately wanted to apologize to him for the mean things she'd said before and

109

although she had no idea where to start, she wanted to talk to him about what he'd found.

The first thing she noticed was the empty couch. Maybe he's in the bathroom, she thought. But as she walked to the back of the dark house, CJ realized no one was there. He was not there. She walked back to the front room and sat on the couch.

I've lost someone else and this time it is my own fault. Lord, what have I done that You keep taking those I love away from me?

That was the closest thing to prayer she could muster as she cried softly at first and then louder as the intensity of the loss consumed her. CJ felt delirious; as though she was in a year-long nightmare and could not wake up. She picked up her journal and pen and tried to write, but this time, she couldn't even gather the strength to channel how she felt onto the page. Hopelessness knocked on the door of her mind until she heard the metal jangling of keys and the click of the door being pushed open.

Casting a six-foot shadow in the dark room lit by only the streetlights that seeped through the ivory, vertical blinds, Jonathan stood in the doorway of the front door and stared at CJ. He hurt for her because he couldn't imagine how she could have held onto such an awful secret for so long. Just like he wouldn't tell her he'd angrily gone to the North side to look for her molester, he also wouldn't tell her he'd been standing outside the door for the last ten minutes listening to her cries and half-prayers. His heart thumped in his chest as he closed the door behind him and sat down next to her on the couch.

CJ couldn't believe she'd questioned his loyalty to her. After all, he came back. He could have left her life forever, but he came back. He could have been ashamed of her and accused her of the same things she'd been accusing herself over the last ten years, but he didn't. He wouldn't. He simply came back, sat down next to her and held her in his arms.

His comfort overwhelmed CJ and the sweetness of the moment took over as she lifted her head and kissed her friend, her *best* friend, on the lips. Realizing what she'd done, CJ pulled back and searched Jonathan's face for any sign of a breach. She didn't see any. In fact, Jonathan returned her kiss with several more urgent ones as he gently held CJ's face in his hands. He then wrapped his hands around her waist and pulled her so close to him, their noses nearly touched and their heated breaths sent the temperature of the room skyrocketing.

"I love you, Cris."

Upon hearing Jonathan's declaration, CJ suddenly pulled away.

"I've always loved you," he continued.

Confused, CJ moved to the end of the couch. Her shift felt to Jonathan like a million ginsu knives piercing his heart.

"You don't believe me? In twenty years, I've never lied to you. Why would I start now?"

"Because you feel sorry for me. For what happened to me."

"Yes, I do feel sorry for what happened to you..."

CJ's face twisted at the thought of his kisses being born of pity.

"...and I love you."

"Why," CJ cried.

"What do you mean...why?"

"Why do you love me? You can have any girl you want. Heck, you've *had* any girl you wanted. How could you love someone like me?"

Jonathan heard her deeper question. The one that questioned her innocence in the matter. The one that confirmed she was to blame for all that had happened to her. Guilt and shame deafened her to his sincerity.

"How could I *not* love someone like you?"

"Not good enough." CJ needed to hear more, but Jonathan had no idea how to put into words his feelings. For his and CJ's sake, he wanted to desperately tell her all of what God had shown him in the hours he wandered the city in search of the man who stole the little girl from him. But because of the weight of his own baggage, he had no idea how to do that.

"You have to leave," CJ announced as she stood up. Jonathan did not move.

111

"Don't do this, CJ. I'm still your friend."

Looking down at him as he remained seated on the couch, CJ fought the urge to reach out and touch again the smoothness of his face.

"I know. But I think I need to be alone."

Though she didn't touch him, Jonathan felt her pull away from him in the worst kind of way.

"Your uncle will be back in town tomorrow night, right?" She said, finally void of any emotion.

"Yes."

"Then stay tonight, but I need you gone by tomorrow."

Jonathan heard his heart break for what seemed like the billionth time.

"Does this mean we're no longer friends?"

Staring back at him, CJ remembered the six-year-old brown boy.

"No."

"No, we're no longer friends or No, it doesn't mean that."

A line had been crossed. They both knew that. But because they'd traveled this far together on their journeys, they also both knew they were forever connected.

"No, it doesn't mean that."

Jonathan finally stood up. His legs felt as heavy as his heart. In spite of the walls put up by their pasts, the heat still crackled between them. CJ took one step back to gain her bearings and then turned around to head to her bedroom. As she walked slowly around the couch, Jonathan moved toward her and gently took hold of her arm. Turning her to face him, he gently placed a kiss on her forehead and then released her. CJ stared back at him. There were no more tears for her to cry and no more uncertainty in what she would do next. The question was when.

Chapter 12

It had been awhile since CJ had gone to the monthly spa days with her Aunt Kara and Aunt Toni. Although she had really begun to deal with the issues around her mother, it was difficult for her to be a part of such a regular celebration of her memory. In addition to that, being around Aunt Kara after the whole Jonathan snooping in her journal thing, made her nervous. She wasn't ready to spill her guts quite yet. Nevertheless, this was the first spa day Aunt Toni was able to attend after completing her last round of chemotherapy and CJ didn't want to miss spending time with her.

Kara, Toni and CJ all sat in pedicure chairs chit chatting about current events and discussing Toni's health.

"You should really take it easy, Toni. You just finished your treatment." Kara looked at her friend with concern.

"Honey, even with one breast, I'm more fabulous than some of these women out here. I'll be just fine."

No one could ever accuse Toni of lacking confidence.

"Girl, you are a mess! I'm going to pray God gives you just a little humbleness," Kara said.

Toni laughed.

"You can pray all you want, but God knows exactly who I am. Who do you think made me this way?"

CJ laughed out loud. She had to admit, if she had half the courage and confidence Toni had, she'd probably have fewer problems.

"That's right, Aunt Toni. You go girl!"

Kara faked a frown.

"Don't encourage her."

Toni knew what her girls expected of her and she was determined to deliver. She'd always been the one to see the silver lining in even the worst situations and although her last bout with cancer left her depressed and wanting to die, she would never show it. She needed to pretend she was on top of things, even if she wasn't sure she was.

For a few moments, each of the three women sat deep in thought as the nail technicians soaked, clipped and rubbed their troubles momentarily out through the soles of their feet. Kara was the first to speak again.

"So, Miss Germaine, is it true you have a special house guest?"

CJ stiffened.

"Where did you hear that?" She said it a little harsher than she'd intended.

Kara looked at Toni knowingly.

"Oooh, calm down, lady. I talked to Cassandra last week and she said you'd come to visit her and told her that Jonathan was back in Chicago. She also said he was staying with you for a while."

That was the terrible thing about having family and friends of family that were so close. Secrets didn't stay secrets for very long. At least some of them, anyway.

"He's not staying with me anymore, but yes, he is back in Chicago."

Toni gave her two cents. "I always liked him for you. Have you guys ever..."

CJ didn't like the direction of the exchange and, without thinking, changed the subject to a matter she'd later regret bringing up.

"...uh, Aunt Kara. How are the divorce proceedings going?"

114

Toni, aware that CJ had switched gears, playfully rolled her eyes at the junior member of the crew.

Aunt Kara answered CJ as she moved from the pedicure chair to the manicure station walking on her heels. "It's really tough. You would have thought I was Joan Collins the way Benson is fighting me for every dollar."

"Well, what do you expect? When you have a baby on the way..." Toni chimed in sarcastically. Kara looked like she'd been struck.

"Aunt Toni!"

Toni immediately regretted her statement.

"Oh, K, I'm so sorry."

"No, it's okay, Toni. It does hurt, but I have to get used to hearing that."

CJ had hoped the conversation was over as the queasiness that resulted from any mention of Benson had started to churn her stomach. Unfortunately, Toni wanted to hear more.

"So, he's fighting you for the townhouse?"

"Yes, girl. He wants to sell it and split the money, but I'm not leaving my home. I'm just not."

"Even though there are so many memories there," Toni said.

CJ had finished her pedicure and for one minute contemplated walking barefoot, on the back of her heals with cotton balls between her toes, right out of the spa. She didn't know if she would be able to bear hearing any more. Why did I ask her about the divorce, she thought. In trying to avoid one sensitive subject, she'd trapped herself in another one that was even touchier. But she couldn't leave. She didn't know how she would be able to get away so abruptly without being questioned so instead, she went to the manicure station and waited the story out. She could not have anticipated what would be said next.

"That's exactly why I want to stay. They're my memories. They're mine. Benson has taken so much from me for fifteen of the thirty years we've been married and I refuse to let him take any more." Kara paused. "Plus..."

115

Kara looked at Toni in search of any softness that would allow her to share her heart right then. Toni smiled at her.

"Plus what?"

"Plus, a part of me believes him when he says that..."

Toni's face changed quickly when she heard the familiar tone of compassion in her friend's voice."

"Don't do it, girl. He doesn't deserve it."

"None of us do, Toni."

CJ watched the two old friends go back and forth. She felt something coming.

"No, Kara. I'm not talking about some *eternalforgivenessbyGodandourinherent unworthinessofHisgraceandmercy.*" She ran the words together as though they were some heavily cited, but barely believed, mantra of the super-saved.

Toni continued. "Don't talk that talk with me. You're not God. You're a woman who has been hurt by her husband. A woman who's husband broke their covenant in exchange for some fling with a child."

CJ tried to stand up quickly, but her knees hit the underside of the manicure station causing water and bottles to go flying. Her stomach bubbled.

Both Kara and Toni turned to CJ.

"Uh. I-I-I'm okay," she said when all she really wanted to do was to disappear into the floor.

Kara turned backed to Toni.

"I know what happened, Toni. I was there, remember! I'm just saying, I think this girl was the first time he ever really cheated on me physically. I know there has been talk about him and other women and I'm sure he's thought about it, but I just don't think he's been with anyone else before this girl. I just can't believe that."

CJ couldn't control the bile that was caught in her throat as Kara shared how she felt about Benson's affair. Caught up in the heat of their conversation, the two women didn't notice as she ran to the restroom just in time to release her lunch into the white bowl.

116

Toni looked at Kara incredulously at first then quickly shifted to pity and later, genuine compassion.

"Whatever makes you feel better, K. Whatever gives you peace."

Peace was exactly what Kara was trying to hold on to, even though it felt a long, long way from where she was.

***

"Ms. Germaine?"

The intern was distinctly Irish with long, crimson hair, reddish-brown freckles that dotted her nose and cheeks, and porcelain skin. With no response from her boss, she followed her knock with a quick peek into the editor's office.

"Ms. Germaine?"

Staring out the window at the dark-blue expanse of Lake Michigan and lost in her thoughts, CJ did not hear the collegian call her name.

"Ms. Germaine, is everything okay?"

No.

"Yes, of course, Rachel."

Once again, she sacrificed the truth for the sake of appearance. The intern didn't buy it, but couldn't think of one thing she could do to help her boss except of course, her job.

"I have New York on the phone. They're asking about the copy for the June feature."

Even with a four-month lead time, she couldn't seem to pull the words together.

"Could you let them know I will have something for them on Friday?"

Her tailored suit, bought for her by her Aunt Toni who always said a successful woman should have a suit that fits her well, led the entire Midwest office of *Epic Magazine,* and anyone else that caught her coming into the office building on Michigan and Wacker, to believe she was a woman in control. But if they looked even a little deeper, they would see her eyes told a different story altogether. Nevertheless, the Irish intern did not question CJ. She simply closed the door and went back to her desk to relay the message.

117

CJ returned to staring at the lake, silently wishing she could throw all that distressed her far into its deepest parts.

***

As much as CJ loved her work at *Epic*, she was actually considering quitting at this point. The weight of her secret had finally stripped her of the passion for writing she used to feel. The pen was no longer her savior. It no longer held the quick fix she needed when the memories were once only fleeting. It used to be that by simply retreating into that special place where words dwelled, she could find glimpses of sunlight in the midst of the darkness. Now, she just felt overwhelmed by her own thoughts and the anticipation of what would eventually come once everything was revealed. If anything, writing was forcing the pain to the surface. Forcing her to either deal with it or hand it over to Someone who could. She didn't feel strong enough to do either. Even though Jonathan knew her story, the distance she'd created between them meant she would not be able to benefit from the love and support he could offer her.

Bottom line? She was officially alone. Passionless, purposeless and yet, still fiercely independent. CJ knew she was the source of all of her pain. Not that she caused it, but because she could not let it go. Because she held it all in, the shame and guilt strangled her soul. She was alone with a heart shot full of holes. Unwilling and unable to surrender it all to the God of her earliest years—the One she dreamt about. It had been a long time since she recalled the dream she had when she was twelve. At least she thought it was a dream. It felt as real as the blankets she wrapped tightly around her body that night. The night Jesus sat down on the edge of her bed.

Adult CJ closed her eyes tightly trying to remember what He looked like. The color of his eyes would not come to her, but she did remember the warmth that emanated from them as He took her hand. His eyes were like a fire, only not the raging kind, but more soft and soothing as she stared back at him in child-like wonderment. If one could feel words, then His were like silk as He quietly spoke to her.

118

Remember.

Even though she was sure it was Him that spoke them, the words didn't really have any sound. It was more like an echo in young CJ's mind and heart. Reclining back into her office chair as though that would crystallize the memory for her, the grown CJ said aloud, "Remember what?"

She could see herself. Hair pulled back into the massive afro-puff she wore her entire seventh-grade year. Eyelashes blinking back the tears that were a result of being surrounded by so much love. Loosening the grip on the blankets, she smiled back at the man whose face shone, even in the blackness of her room.

No matter what you do. No matter what is done to you. I love you.

Grown-up CJ wasn't so sure about that, even if the little girl believed it wholeheartedly. Too much had happened between now and then. It was much easier, though to seek solace in the memory.

My love is greater than any hurt you'll ever know.

Both CJs wondered whether He meant the pain was over or that there was more to come.

Trust me.

She promised Him she would never forget His words and yet, when adult CJ opened her eyes and checked back into reality, she realized she had. Until that very moment, she'd forgotten.

***

That's the funny thing about forgetting God's promises. It doesn't make them any less true, but it does make it harder to give up the things we've replaced our trust in Him with, especially when the time comes to surrender everything and go back to the place where He first spoke to us. For CJ, that meant going back to that little girl who received His love so graciously. She didn't think she could do it. Too much was at stake. Her father. The mother figures in her life. Her career. Any hope for true love. Her sanity. Not that she believed she was worthy of any of those things anyway.

Chapter 13

While Langston looked forward to his retirement party, CJ dreaded it. Her dad's party wasn't going to be the type of occasion one would expect for a highly respected, tenured professor. The kind where colleagues and friends ate a few finger sandwiches, toasted the honoree and wished him well, all within the span of a couple of hours. Langston had given his life to his work as an educator and college administrator, and so for him, it was fitting to invite every single person who played a part in his success to an all-night celebration of his career.

CJ stood in the doorway of her father's home office holding the guest list for the party.

"Both of them, Dad? Are you serious?"

Langston did not have to guess what his daughter was referring to and by the incredulous look in her eyes he didn't have to guess how she felt about it either. He didn't respond.

Not to be ignored, CJ walked across the room and leaned over his desk.

"I know you hear me."

Langston looked up from his laptop and smiled.

"Yes, my sweet, beautiful, understanding daughter. I did hear you."

CJ folded her arms. Her frustration would not allow her to buy his sweet talk.

"No, Daddy, don't even try it."

Langston loved to watch her get mad. It was like someone had put his entire life on rewind stopping and playing at the best part. She was definitely Sasha's daughter.

"How could you invite Benson AND Aunt Kara to the party?"

"Because I want them to come."

Could he be more selfish, CJ thought, although she would never actually say that.

"They are getting a divorce, Dad. A DIVORCE!"

CJ plopped down in the leather recliner that sat next to multiple shelves fill with books. She felt like she wanted to cry, but she refused. She'd shed enough tears over the last few months to last her forever.

Langston looked over at his daughter and noticed how her face seemed to be etched with pain. He finally turned completely away from his laptop. Playing nonchalant wasn't going to work this time. CJ had been through so much lately and while his intentions were genuine in wanting Kara and Benson to be together in the same room and maybe remember their love for each other, he didn't want to add to his daughter's stress. He'd promised his wife, even as she lay on her death bed, that he would do everything he knew how to do to protect their beautiful baby girl from any hurt or harm, or he would die trying. And for a long time, Langston believed he'd done just that. However, in that moment as CJ stared blankly at the ceiling in his office, he saw the great sorrow held captive in the beautiful, nearly-black eyes and something tore at him. Now, he wasn't so sure.

***

The party started off pretty well. Music from the eighties and the nineties filled the air. Although CJ was on the verge of nausea from listening to one too many songs by New Edition and the Gap Band, it warmed her to see her father having a good time. He'd worked hard for the university and had reaped great professional successes, even in the face of his great personal trials. During the evening, a toast was given by friends and colleagues celebrating her dad and lightly roasting him about their many run-in's with Dr. Germaine as well as his other quirks. CJ laughed along with everyone else, knowing most of what was said was right, even if a bit exaggerated. Forgetting for a moment the many elephants in the room, she found herself caught up in the glow of the moment. Langston winked at his only daughter from across the room, something he used to do when she was a little girl and performing on a stage for some school or church program. It was his way of comforting her anxiety and it always worked. That moment was no exception. CJ was genuinely proud of him. She hoped this party would be everything he hoped for, but silently, her heart ached because she knew in more than one way, it wouldn't be.

After the mini-program and Langston's long, semi-emotional speech, most of his professional friends, colleagues from the university and members of the church, said their goodbyes and headed home. Left in the room were close family and friends who, feeling a little bit more free since the stuffy folks had left, began to eat the incredible meal prepared by Kara and cut a rug to the oldies but goodies. No one noticed the lines, though. Imaginary lines drawn to keep everyone boxed in and comfortable in their own safe zones. The lines were only obvious to those who knew the back stories of the guests. Those who knew how to see beyond the tightness of the smiles and the shortness of the laughter.

CJ saw the lines. Was too familiar with them. She watched as Aunt Kara and Aunt Toni two-stepped in their invisible box over by the buffet table. She also watched as two of the young men her dad mentored laughed loudly in theirs. As though he'd been punished like a child who'd messed up too many times, Benson sat in another unseen box over in the corner by the stereo, careful to not make eye contact with anyone other than Langston. For CJ, it frustrated her that she was the only one that overlapped, moving freely from one box to the next with the exception of Benson's. She pretended to belong to each of them, even though she knew she was only the link between them all. A broken one, but a link

122

nonetheless. It also made her even more upset that her father was oblivious to it.

Langston didn't seem to notice his friends, the ones he'd so desperately wanted to see together again, were not actually together. In fact, they were further apart than they'd ever been. The only thing that seemed common to them all was his daughter and the pressure of that burden seemed to be getting the best of CJ. She felt almost schizophrenic— moving too quickly between feelings of great joy and love for her father and his accomplishments to an even greater sadness at the fragmented relationships surrounding them. She prayed she would not breakdown.

On top of all the invisible boundaries she saw and felt that evening, CJ had her own lines and box to consider. One major one was Jonathan. Langston invited him because he didn't know what had transpired between them and neither of them had any plans to tell him. Yet, it was moments like these, when the pressure of isolation and shame seemed to strangle her that she wished she had her friend to talk her down from the ledge she'd climbed. Jonathan knew this also. His eyes never left CJ during the entire party as he watched her move back and forth between each corner of the room. Early in the evening, he'd also noticed how people had blocked themselves off. To the untrained eye, it would appear as though everyone was mingling well. Even Langston seemed unaware. Yet, Jonathan was also privy to the back story and watched from his own solitary box as various groups gathered together around the fire of their familiarity and how CJ moved carefully, as though she was considering the consequence of every single step she made, between each clique. There was only one side of the room she didn't dare venture. The one where Benson sat solemnly staring at the bottom of his glass filled with cranberry juice. There's no doubt he was wishing there was something a little more clear and much more potent to go with the blood-red juice.

Jonathan's eyes turned back to CJ who was staring at him. Her eyes pierced his heart. In the moment before she quickly turned away from him, he heard her. He heard her

123

heart, though torn and weary, even though no sound left her mouth. An appeal wrapped tightly around an accusation. She needed him, but her pride wouldn't let her say so. That was okay, though. Jonathan had never been a fan of her pride anyway. As CJ darted onto the balcony of her father's town home, she looked out onto a quieter section of the normally bustling 53rd Street. She didn't see Jonathan as he slipped outside behind her. Her tears were not noticeable to anyone but him.

"Hey, Cris."

Though CJ hadn't heard him follow her outside, somewhere deep down inside she knew he'd be there. It was just their way.

"Hey."

Jonathan approached her cautiously.

"Are you okay?"

She could have lied. She could have explained away her emotions as a response to how great the party was and how proud she was of her dad. But CJ was tired of lying.

"No."

"I know things have been strange between us since..."

CJ put her hands up, stopping him mid-sentence.

"Let's not go there, okay?"

"C, we have to go there! We have to talk about it!"

"Why?"

That was hard. He didn't fully know why.

He decided on a different approach.

"Listen. I'm going to be honest. There is a part of me that would love to run away from you. From this. But I can't. I have never been able to run away from you and I'm surely not going to run away from you now..."

He paused to gauge her stability.

"...especially knowing what I know."

CJ's face was suddenly stricken with panic.

"Don't do this. Not today. I can't bare to think about that today."

Jonathan became frustrated. He moved closer to CJ who'd tried to turn away, but was trapped in place where the iron railings kissed and gave birth to a corner.

"Think about what? Think about the awful thing you had to endure? Is that what you're afraid of thinking about?"

CJ's mind felt like it was melting. One thought merged with another and another until she felt overwhelmed by her emotions. She lashed out.

"I wasn't totally innocent, you know? I let it happen."

This hurt Jonathan the most. The fact that she believed she was at fault for what happened to her. She was the one that had been sinned against. She was the one who'd been taken advantage of, but she was the only one who seemed to be living with the guilt and shame of it all.

"What do you mean you let it happen to you? You were fifteen!"

He couldn't stop himself from putting the truth out there. Maybe by speaking it aloud, it would free her, he thought.

"It's not your fault! You were only fifteen years old, a child, when you were violated by your father's so-called best friend!"

CJ eyes changed. Became blank and unwritten. He couldn't read her response except that she was no longer staring at him but beyond him, over his shoulder.

Jonathan couldn't have known that Langston, although enjoying his party, was still concerned about the one woman left in his life he loved more than anything. Jonathan couldn't have known that after noticing CJ had left the party, Langston would go searching for his daughter. He surely didn't know Langston would be standing behind him when those awful words were given life.

Jonathan followed CJ's frozen eyes to the figure behind him.

"Mr. Germaine, I..."

Jonathan might as well have not been standing there. Langston looked directly at his daughter with angry tears fighting their way to his eyes.

"Is...this...true...CJ?"

Every bit of emotion Langston had buried in his soul for the last thirty years came forward in that moment. Leading the way was an incensing, passionate anger. An anger that, late or not, would do anything to protect his child.

CJ couldn't move. She didn't want to respond to her father. She'd never wanted him to find out this way. She wasn't sure she wanted him to find out at all. But, he had and if there was one thing she knew about her dad, he was not going to let this go until she responded.

Broken, she spoke. "Daddy, I..."

"Is this true?" His eyes searched the face of his beloved. For the first time in his life, he actually hoped she was lying to him. That would be so much easier to deal with than the truth.

Jonathan stepped back into focus and took CJ's hand.

Speaking softly, he said, "It's time. Tell him."

"Yes," CJ responded in barely a whisper.

One lone tear slipped from Langston's right eye. He was not concerned anymore that it was his retirement party. He didn't care that his friends and family were there to celebrate him. He could care less even if any church folk had hung around looking for a little drama. In that moment, the only thing he cared about was retribution for his child and by default, her mother. He remembered the promise he made that day so long ago.

Turning around with fists balled tightly, Langston, with his long, powerful stride, walked swiftly back into the living room with CJ and Jonathan on his heels. For a second, CJ noticed the imaginary boxes were gone. Freed maybe, by the truth.

Langston spotted Benson trying to talk to an unyielding Kara. Benson's back was turned away from the fury that sped towards him. Only Kara saw the look on Langston's face and heard that sweet, small Voice tell her to step back. She did. She stepped back just enough for Langston to wrap his arm around the neck of his ex-friend in the clothes hanger wrestling move they used to playfully perform on each other in college. Only this time, it wasn't a joke. Langston tried to squeeze every bit of life out of Benson, just like he could only imagine this secret had done to his daughter.

Benson was able to pop loose from his grip momentarily, but Langston was a freight train moving full speed ahead. It was as if no one else was in the room. His wrath was endless as he punched and punched continuously. His swings were wild and controlled all at the same time.

Benson didn't have a chance to think as each fist connected to his jaws and eyes and head. He tried to scream. To get Langston's attention.

"What is your problem, man?"

Finally, they were parted by a few of the men in the room. Langston, filled with maddening frustration, finally responded to Benson's questions.

"What's my problem? My problem is you! But not for long..."

Langston moved toward Benson again, but the wall of chests and arms that stood in front of him held him back. He heard a Voice that sounded like it came from above his head say what he already knew, *"Revenge is mine."* But this time, he chose not listen. He could not allow this to happen again. Whether it was by killing the spirit or killing the flesh, no one was going to take from him another woman he loved. Not on his watch.

Kara stepped between the two men and the group of men who were holding them back.

"Langston, my God, what is going on?"

She considered it might have been that he was angry Benson was trying to talk to her. Maybe he misread her response to her husband's tugging of her arm as being afraid. But, on the other hand, it was Langston who invited them both to the party, so he couldn't have been too surprised there would be some kind of dialogue.

"Why don't you ask him, K?"

CJ walked into the center of the commotion still holding Jonathan's hand. Jon was still whispering words of strength to his friend.

127

"It's time."

"Get free."

"I know it hurts, but turn it loose."

Benson looked at CJ and then back at Langston as it suddenly dawned on him what had come to light. Exposed, he dropped his head.

"Don't do that," Langston yelled. "Don't act ashamed now! You weren't ashamed then!"

Kara trembled as she stared at CJ still trying to figure out what was happening, but frightened by what was being implied.

Benson spoke slowly. "Wait a minute, man. Let me explain."

Langston frustrated himself more as he tried unsuccessfully to lunge toward Benson again.

"Explain what? How can you possibly explain having sex with my fifteen-year-old daughter?"

The pain shot through Kara's chest as though she'd been physically punched. She slumped down in the chair behind her, sobbed loudly then just as quickly, looked up at CJ for confirmation. Her words were chopped by her grief.

"What...are...they...talking...about?"

CJ's eyes were as round as saucers. No words would come to her.

Kara's voice grew louder and more urgent as she stood up and faced the girl she loved like her own daughter.

"WHAT...ARE...THEY...TALKING...ABOUT?"

Jonathan squeezed CJ's hand tighter. To let her know he was there. That nothing else would happen to her.

"When I was fifteen..."

CJ's tone spoke the truth even before her words did.

"I was watching Mari and Anthony..."

Langston cut in.

"...when this piece of trash molested her!!"

Kara fell back onto the couch. Her eyes closed. She prayed the Lord would take her right then. But He didn't.

Benson raged. "Are you serious, CJ? Molested? Really? You never stopped me from massaging you!"

128

His accusation shattered CJ. This time, Jonathan let go of her hand and started toward Benson. However, another man, a friend of Langston's from the church, stepped between him and his target.

CJ mentally disconnected from that moment and began to mutter to herself, "I was fifteen. I was a virgin. I didn't know. I thought..."

Kara came to and tried to stand up again. She wanted to go over to CJ and tell her she didn't blame her, that she still loved her and that it wasn't her fault. But she couldn't. She couldn't bring herself to do that and she was ashamed of it.

"Of course you didn't know..." In the past, Langston would have caught and commented on CJ's use of the word "was" when speaking of her virginity, but this time, he didn't. He only had one mission in mind and that was hurting the man who took her innocence.

He continued. "...you were fifteen years old. This man took advantage of you and I'm about to take advantage of him!"

Benson saw in Langston's eyes the same pain he'd saw when Sasha died. He tried to recant, in hopes he could escape his friend's wrath.

"Listen, man. I'm sorry. I was drinking heavily back then. Even dabbling with drugs..."

Kara shrieked at this news.

"...everything was crazy. I'd lost my job..."

No excuse sounded reasonable to Langston, so Benson, with a blackness that blinded his heart and mind, went back to his accusations.

"Whatever! She wanted it man. I promise you she did."

CJ collapsed in Jonathan's arms. As everyone focused on the two women, they left an opening for Langston. Finally free from the arms that held him at bay, he rushed Benson, pushing him against the wall. Stepping back, Langston reached back to swing, but this time, Benson was anticipating the hit and grabbed Langston's arm and twisted it behind his back. As another group of men in the room ran over to pull

129

the men apart, Benson shoved Langston away from him with all of his strength.

His intentions were simply to get Langston off of him. Somewhere deep down, he understood Langston's anger, but former friend or not, he wasn't going to let him beat him down. Especially since he'd beat himself down enough for both of them over the last decade.

When Benson pushed Langston, he fell face forward. Jonathan and the others, assuming that Langston would catch his balance, grabbed Benson and pinned him against the wall before he could retaliate more. Everyone, however, turned when they heard the crash. Langston's head sat awkwardly on his neck after smashing onto the corner of the large glass end table. CJ screamed and leaped forward toward her father. His eyes, like the final curtain in a play, closed slowly. The last picture in the frame of his life was that of his daughter.

"DADDY!"

Chapter 14

The wrinkled funeral program that sat on the edge of the wooden coffee table read:

Langston Germaine
1972 – 2031
Husband. Father. Friend.

Everyday life was enough evidence for CJ that God existed. The sun, the rain, the moon, the stars were all the fruit of His creation. Seasons changing. Leaves shedding their bright green garments in exchange for gold or red or brown ones. These were her reminders that God existed. At nearly thirty years old, it wasn't an issue of whether she believed in God. She was just far from being His fan. Actually, that's an understatement. She didn't like Him at all.

CJ was familiar with all of the theological arguments around the question of why bad things happen to good people. She'd wrestled with that a while ago, when she'd first tasted hurt and pain. The fact was those theories only appealed to her hunger for discourse and debate. They never reached her heart and they certainly didn't satisfy her soul now that her entire world had been shattered. The hole that already existed had now grown wider and she firmly believed that it, nor she, would ever be filled. CJ also couldn't help to wonder how an all-powerful, all-knowing, all-loving God allowed her life to turn out the way it had?

Sitting on the oversized sofa in her living room, CJ still wore the same clothes she wore to her father's funeral the day before. She repeatedly flicked the remote in search of mind-numbing entertainment that would help her escape the thoughts and feelings that sat ready to consume her. Unfortunately, not one of the 800 channels could quench her desire for distraction. She closed her eyes and considered happier times.

***

When CJ was six, she always wondered whether adults were really big and strong or just appeared that way because she was so small. She had a habit of testing the strength of her dad by sneaking up on him and punching her tiny fist into the meaty part of his calf.

"Aayyyyahhh!"

The hard muscle would not give as the little girl would try again.

"Aayyyyahhhhhh!"

Langston looked down at this little Bruce Lee.

"And what are you doing, Missy?"

CJ would give her father the biggest, brightest smile she could muster before announcing her intentions.

"I'm going to chop your leg off!"

Langston chuckled.

"And why would you want to do that?"

That was a hard question for CJ. She didn't really want to chop his leg off. It was just fun to pretend that she could.

Langston watched his little girl ponder his question as though he'd asked her what was the square root of pie. He laughed again, this time louder.

"So you think you are strong, huh?"

CJ perked up. She knew she was strong.

"I know I am strong!"

"Okay. Let's see about that."

Langston rolled up the sleeve of his right arm to expose a bicep that, to CJ, looked absolutely massive. Bending down a bit, he flexed his arm. CJ's eyes bulged as she stared at her dad as though he was Superman. Langston glowed under the admiration of his child. CJ grabbed the muscles with both hands, one on each side, and interlocked her fingers. Pulling with all her might, she tried to remain planted on the ground by pulling down on her dad's arm. Langston let CJ struggle for a moment and even allowed her to remain flat-footed for a while. He wanted to encourage her; teaching her to believe anything's possible.

Finally, after he felt CJ's hands loosen with the beginnings of exhaustion, Langston lifted CJ from the ground while she was still holding his bicep. The little girl giggled as her feet became airborne and she dangled from her dad's arm. He was the strongest man she knew and knowing he could carry her with one arm led her to believe he would always be there to lift her up when she couldn't do it herself.

Of course, that was before…

***

Against the little bit of will she had left, CJ felt herself being pulled from the shelter of her memory and back to the harsh reality of consciousness. She used the back of her hand to clear the blurry mucus that had formed over her eyes. Regaining her focus, she stared at the television as words that sounded much like the answers she refused to accept were being hurled from the screen by a heavy, almond-colored man donning a blue-black suit and a red tie.

"Some of us got it twisted. God is not always in our lives to save us from hard times. Sometimes, He allows trials and tribulations to happen in order to teach us something. Sometimes, He has to teach us to reach us. Sometimes, He has to break us to make us. Sometiiiiimes, He has to hold us to mold us into who He has called us to be. So we can depend and put our trust solely in Him."

The anger returned. CJ didn't want to hear the Spirit that spoke behind the words. To her, it was all garbage.

Church rhetoric meant to pacify the ignorance of those who'd forsaken any accountability in their lives. She wasn't going for it. CJ reached for the remote, but couldn't seem to find it in the place where she last remembered holding it. Meanwhile, the preacher continued.

"Just like Job, God will allow His hedge to be loosened from around us, so we can be tested. God loves us so much that He will allow us to be stripped completely in order for us to get free and live our lives filled with..."

Click.

She'd had enough. CJ refused to rationalize her situation as an act of God on her behalf. That made no sense to her. Actually, she didn't even know if it was an act of the Devil. In her mind, she'd done all of this to herself.

The buzz from her cell phone startled her as she sat up for the first time in 18 hours. It was Jonathan. He'd been calling every hour on the hour since they'd left the repast. She didn't particularly care to answer it, but she also needed something to divert her attention from the television preacher's sermon that still rang deafeningly in her spirit. She picked up the phone to answer, even though she'd already decided to only half-listen to him. Holding the phone tightly between her shoulder and cheek, she perused the mail that was stacked on the coffee table.

"How can I help you?" CJ's voice was void of emotion, as though she were speaking to a bill collector and not her best friend. Jonathan's relief could almost be felt through the phone as he sighed loudly.

"Oh my goodness! I have been calling you..."

CJ interrupted, "Yeah, I know. At least twenty times..."

Jon knew CJ was talking from her place of pain and so he chose to ignore her tone and sarcasm.

"How are you?"

"How would you expect me to be?"

134

"Listen, Cris. I'm just concerned about you. I just wanted to make sure you were okay."

"Yeah, join the club."

Once again, Jonathan ignored her curt response.

"Have you eaten? Do you want to go get some dinner?"

The last thing she wanted to do was sit in front of Jonathan pretending to eat. Pretending to care. She flipped quickly through the stack of mail until she came across a letter from the Calypso Writer's Foundation and the Universidade do Estado da Bahia. She used the letter opener she kept on top of the refrigerator to carefully cut open the envelope. Reading it quickly, the letter said she'd been awarded a six-month writing fellowship in the Brazilian haven of Salvador de Bahia. The fellowship would start in a month. She'd almost forgotten she'd even applied for it and now, here it was. Her ticket away from her despair. The first pleasant thought she'd had in weeks crossed her mind. The second thought was not so pleasant. She recalled the elaborate stories her father used to tell her about his fantasy honeymoon with her mother in Bahia.

"Hellooooooo!" Jonathan yelled from the line.

CJ had almost forgotten he was on the phone.

"So, do you want to get something to eat?"

"I don't think so. Plus, you're all the way on the north side. It's going to take forever for you to get here."

It was Jonathan's turn to pause. "Actually…"

She heard a knock at the door.

"Hold on."

CJ walked slowly to the door ignoring what her instincts were telling her. When she opened the door, Jonathan stood there holding his cell phone up to his ear. His smile, while tentative, was gorgeous as ever; made brighter after seeing that CJ was safe and home.

"So, you've been outside of my door this whole time?"

CJ was perturbed by this. She didn't want to deal with him. After glaring at him a few minutes, she stepped aside and let him into the apartment.

"Well, I told you. When you didn't pick up the phone, I got concerned. So after the *fifteenth* try, I got in my car and drove here. Then, I saw your car outside and thought maybe I should call one more time before breaking your door down."

Jonathan looked around as though he expected someone else to be there, even though the idea of someone other than himself comforting CJ made his heart drop. No he's not trying to act jealous, CJ thought.

"You thought I had someone in here? Sorry, babe. That's *your* modus operandi, not mine."

Jonathan's smile vanished. "Ouch."

Feeling comfortable in her meanness, she continued. "I'm not like you. I don't ease my pain by wallowing between the legs of some random woman."

Jonathan felt the prick of each verbal stab, but still refused to give in to her negativity, even if it meant listening to her throw his long-abandoned past in her face.

"Well, I hope not with a woman."

CJ rolled her eyes. "Don't try to be funny. You know what I mean!"

They stood there staring at each other. CJ walked over to the couch and picked up the letter she'd been reading and placed it into her purse.

"There is no solace…none…found in a man."

That saddened Jonathan, but he remained persistent.

"So, are you hungry?"

Exasperated, CJ took off the jacket to the black suit she'd worn to the funeral. She pushed it into Jonathan's face, making sure he got a whiff of the day-old funk that lingered in the lining.

"Uhhh, isn't it quite obvious that I'm not ready to go anywhere?"

Jonathan took the jacket out of CJ's hand and placed it neatly on the back of the sofa. If CJ thought her being mean and ornery or repeatedly insulting him or her having not showered in almost two days would send him running back out the front door, she was very much mistaken. Jonathan looked at the wounded woman standing in front of him and said the truest statement that would ever leave his lips.

"It's okay. I'll wait for you."

***

Jonathan could not believe what he was hearing.

"I think I'm going to take it."

"You're actually going to go to Brazil?"

"Yeah, why not?"

He thought he would break down at that point, but he didn't. He was too surprised.

"Ms. Cassie said it might be a good idea for me to get away."

Jonathan still sat in stunned silence. CJ kept talking in hopes that he would cut her off, maybe plead with her to not go.

"Plus, there's nothing left for me here anyway."

Jon's eyes finally lifted from the spot on his plate he'd focused on in order to keep his emotions in check.

"What do you mean 'there's nothing here for you'?"

"I mean just what I said."

"So what am I?"

CJ sighed. Yeah, she wanted him to beg her to stay, but she knew she'd go anyway. That wasn't fair to him.

"You are, and will always be, my friend."

"But what if I want...'

CJ looked up at him and finished his sentence.

"...and what if I don't?"

"How can you say that? I told you how I feel about you."

CJ looked away from him. The conflict was too much for her. She didn't blame Jonathan at all for what happened to her dad. Even when she wanted to, she couldn't. But because she did blame herself, she didn't think she could ever deserve his love, either.

"I know. But I'm a mess and you don't deserve a mess."

Jonathan became frustrated.

137

"So you know what I need now?"

"No. But I do know what *I* need."

Jonathan, heartbroken and angry, dropped the conversation. It was settled. She was going and there was nothing he could do about it. Except pray.

CJ accepted the writer's fellowship in Bahia. An opportunity of a lifetime, the timing of the fellowship seemed almost too perfect. She gave up her editorial position at *Epic* and had officially taken a sabbatical from her career. Everyone, including her boss, said it was probably best she did, as the emotional rollercoaster that had become her life had began to affect her work.

***

Although she knew she was going to have to face Chicago again, spending the next six months in another country felt like a new start. Everything she'd lost over the previous two years could be placed in a much better perspective when you're watching the most beautiful species' of birds dip high and low against the backdrop of a baby-blue sky. When you could find solitude watching a white-sand beach disappear and reappear with the daily tide.

Her accommodations were as simple as her obligations. She stayed in a guesthouse that sat half a mile from the beach in a section of town called Pelourinho. The only thing the fellowship required her to do was write. There were two other fellows staying in the cabin with her. One was a too-laid-back Cuban screenwriter from Houston named Pedro. The other was Ms. Layla, a sixty-year old, African-American novelist from Phoenix who said she was there to resurrect a once-acclaimed writing career. The three shared a common space that included a kitchen and sitting area. Each had their own bedroom and bathroom.

CJ was still angry. She was still sad. She was still hardened by all that had transpired. However, when the plane touched down at Magalhaes Airport, she felt like the cloud that had constantly hovered over her had shifted somehow. Still there, but different. Her plan was to simply write her pain down without concern about rules or structure. This would be the unedited, unrestricted version of her story, which would require her to fill the page with her memories, even if it hurt to recall them. Her thinking? If the truth shall make you free, then she would leave Bahia as free as those birds she watched each morning before breakfast.

The fact that she didn't know anyone didn't frighten CJ at all. In fact, she thought it was excellent preparation for what would ultimately end up being her life anyway. For her, having no one to answer to and no one to please felt good. It was just her and her alone. Not her and God because she'd long tried to sever that relationship after her father's death. Just Crystal Justine Germaine. All by herself. Or so she thought.

***

Anger and Shame are nasty friends. Not only do they consume a person, but they also clear a path for a much more insidious disruption in their lives. CJ was wallowing too deep in her anguish to see what was coming.

Chapter 15

Even though he was a minister, no one could deny the swagger and charm that seemed to be innate to Rev. Noah Alexander. His walk was confident. His talk was profound, if not prophetic, and his eyes smoldered with a kind of deep understanding that kept those who followed his ministry captivated by his every word. So many people found themselves saying, "There's something about him!" and even more found their lives forever changed by some great word that flowed almost effortlessly from his mouth.

On the flipside, there were those who called him arrogant and believed the over-the-top bravado that sometimes seeped out when he dealt with his staff was a sign his so-called "anointing" was just a false spirit that covered great insufficiencies and even greater insecurities. Traits that otherwise would be laid bare if it wasn't for his even greater ability to address the basic needs of his audience. But these naysayers were in the minority. Most folks regarded Rev. Noah very simply as a charismatic preacher with a whole lot to say about the way the world treated the "least of these." This was certainly not a bad thing in and of itself. In any case, he was admired by people near and far for his missions work in South America and after a week of being in Bahia, CJ couldn't help but hear mention of this man and his ministry from just about every local she'd met.

"God is doing great things for His people!"

A combination of Portuguese *Sim's,* Spanish *Si's,* and English *Amen's* filled the air, giving new meaning to speaking in tongues.

"The only thing He requires of you is that you believe. Your faith is what makes you whole."

Another rousing praise went up.

"Remember the woman with the issue of blood?"

"Sim!" "Yes!"

"She had an issue!"

"Si!"

"We all have issues, right?"

"Right!"

"But what did she do? She pressed her way through the crowd. How many of you have had to press your way through!"

"Me."

"Me, too."

"She pressed her way through and believed that if she could just touch the hem of Jesus' garment she'd be healed."

"How many of you have that kind of faith? That outrageous, right-now kind of faith!"

"I do."

"So do I."

"Well, stand up and give God some praise. Praise Him like you believe Him. Praise Him like all you need is the hem of his garment."

The tent service was held in Liberdade in what locals called Lower City, one of the more impoverished areas of the state. Two groups were in attendance at the service. The first were Spiritists, who'd held on to the religion of their ancestors and had worshipped the Orisha, or the gods of West Africa. They were driven to the service by the energy of the worship that was so reminiscent of their own services and yet were held there by the foreign idea of there being only one God. The other group was life-long Catholics that were skeptical of this charismatic form of Christianity and yet were also drawn to the services' powerful preaching and singing. To CJ, it looked like Rev. Noah had them all on the verge of conversion.

As Rev. Noah's words seemed to fill the tent, many in the crowd stood up at once and began clapping their hands, stomping their feet and dancing in the aisle. Some of the regulars laid prostrate at the makeshift altar that had been built at the front of the tent. The atmosphere was charged as the worship reached a fever pitch.

CJ was definitely attracted to the service; at least the spectacle of it. She found herself fascinated by how people could have such a blind faith in an unseen God. Sure, it was familiar to her. She could not possibly forget about those times when she was a child and shared her own child-like trust in Him. Yet, in that moment, she didn't feel privy to the secret they all seemed to share. The secret that fed their belief. All she knew was that the people in that tent prayed earnestly. They were seeking something and this man, this preacher, seemed to have the answer.

It pricked something in her as she watched the mothers and fathers with their children stand in line waiting to be prayed over by the "man of God." It reminded her of her Aunt Kara and the bottle of olive oil she kept in her purse. 'Anointing Oil,' she called it.

"So much it did for her," CJ whispered to herself.

As she stared at the bodies that had fallen in slow motion to the ground after being only briefly touched by the hands of the preacher, she couldn't deny that her spirit was being pulled. In what direction, though, she was not certain.

With her heart beating in sync with the frenetic rhythms of the drummer who provided the soundtrack to the service, CJ desperately wanted to escape the emotions that were building up inside of her and so she did what she did best. She wrote. Slowly at first then faster and faster, CJ dumped everything she thought and felt onto the pages of the leather-bound journal she always carried with her. After releasing her own madness, she turned the attention of her pen to the service. She wrote about the young, Portuguese-speaking mother with rich, brown skin and large, walnut-shaped eyes, who sat two rows ahead of her earlier and who was now spread out, face down, on the ground. Two elderly women, whose faces were lined like maps, stood on either side of the woman, waving fans over her head and consoling her children who obviously had not seen Mommy *slain* before and didn't like it too much. CJ also wrote about the last man standing in the prayer line whose eyes spoke of hunger even before one ever noticed the frailty of his frame.

The preacher continued his loud praying, speaking with a vibrato that seemed to resonate throughout the crowd and calling out for more to come to the altar. CJ matched the urgency of his call by writing so feverishly that her pen broke through the pages on multiple occasions.

Three hours later, the service came to a formal end, despite the fact that many people were still standing around praying and talking with each other. CJ closed her journal and stood up. She headed to the back of the tent somewhat relieved that the experience was over and yet feeling like she couldn't leave. The reporter in her wanted to interview every single person in that tent to get a sense of what moved them so powerfully, as if the sweat on her own brow and the ink on her hands weren't answers enough.

As she followed a group of people who were walking along the same small road that led back to the open air taxi that would take her back to her guesthouse, CJ saw two men with ruddy complexions and dressed in black suits approaching her. Her first thought was that they were brothers.

"M'am?"

"M'am?"

CJ never stopped walking. She clearly remembered the instructions of the program coordinator to never go anywhere alone; to always take a partner. She wished she had listened.

Surprised she didn't stop when they called out to her, the two men turned around and caught up with CJ, each walking alongside her. She gripped her journal and keys tighter, unnerved about their sudden close proximity.

143

She felt a hand graze her elbow and her body went cold. She jumped.

"M'am. I'm sorry. I didn't mean to scare you," said one red-brown brother.

"You were just moving so fast," said the other.

CJ stopped and considered her options. No one walking by them seemed to notice anything was wrong. Maybe it was nothing. The taller brother broke her train of thought.

"Rev. Noah would like to speak with you."

CJ was stunned to hear the name of the preacher. She wasn't aware he'd known who she was much less known she was there.

"And why is that?"

They didn't answer her. Just repeated what they said before.

"Rev. Noah would just like a moment of your time."

CJ vaguely heard the whisper of something telling her to keep walking toward the guesthouse, but she'd grown tired of that Voice and decided to listen to her own.

"Okay."

She followed them toward a smaller tent that sat behind the pulpit of the first. When she walked inside, she quickly noticed a chill, almost like a wind had passed, as her body responded by raising goosebumps along her arms. This was strange to CJ since it was 85 degrees and by no means cold in there. In fact, the air was very stale. She looked up and her eyes met his. For a moment, it felt like hypnosis although she believed she was under no spell. Nevertheless, she became lost in his chestnut-brown pools of sincerity.

"Ms. Germaine?"

She was startled he knew her name until she noticed he held a six-month old copy of *Epic Magazine*. She looked back at him and noticed the sincerity she thought she saw a moment before had dissipated. Suspicion took its place.

"While everyone is welcome to our services, we've had problems with reporters in the past."

He looked down at the journal she was still clutching to make sure she understood his implication.

CJ smiled.

"Oh."

She really couldn't think of anything to say. Technically, she was a reporter, but she wasn't here on any business.

Rev. Noah continued. "Anything you want to know, feel free to ask me directly."

She caught...and ignored...the look that passed between the two brothers who stood guard behind the preacher.

CJ stammered her response. "I-I-I'm sorry. You are mistaken. I'm not a reporter. I mean, I am a reporter. But...But...not today. Not for the next six months."

The preacher raised one eyebrow. He wasn't convinced.

"Uhh...right now, right now I'm a writer on a fellowship with the Calypso Foundation and the Universidade do Estado da Bahia. I stay in Pelourinho. Working on my book."

With teeth as perfect and as white as a winter's first snow, Rev. Noah smiled. CJ cast her head down, knowing her weakness for a beautiful set of teeth.

"I'm sorry, sister," he said. "I just saw you writing so intently during the service, I assumed you were another journalist trying to make a name for yourself by misconstruing what we do down here."

Admittedly, she was interested in what she saw in the service, but not for the reasons he thought.

"It's okay. I understand why you might have thought that."

They both stood there staring at each other for more than a minute past comfortable. Finally, CJ broke the trance.

"I guess I better leave now."

Just as she passed both brothers and nearly reached the exit, she heard Rev. Noah's voice, this time deeper and seemingly echoing off the curtained walls.

"You've had great pain in your life."

The jolt that shook her body stopped her in her tracks. She remained facing away from the three men. Prophecy was common in the churches she'd grown up in, but she'd never had it come to her so directly and she'd always suspected some of the so-called prophets were no different than the fake psychics she'd see on television.

"God is going to use this experience to bring you back to Him."

CJ wasn't too sure about that and decided his words were nothing more than a vague, if precise, perception made by a too-attractive and even more intimidating South American by way of Los Angeles missionary slash preacher.

CJ turned around and smiled her own big, albeit anxious, smile and then quickly made her way out the tent and down the road to the taxi stop.

**

Pushing open the door to the guesthouse, CJ found Ms. Layla eating a small meal she'd prepared. Layla was the self-appointed cook of the house and would often go to town to pick up seafood and other South American specialties to serve the other two fellows. To CJ, it seemed like the old woman spent more time in the kitchen cooking than she did writing and this evening was no different.

CJ smiled at Ms. Layla. There was something about the lady that both unnerved her as well as comforted her. She couldn't really put her finger on it, so sitting down across from her at the table, CJ decided to spark up a conversation to find out.

"How's writing going?"

Ms. Layla looked over at the young woman.

"Pretty good, sugah. Outlining right now. That's how I do it."

"Yeah?" CJ responded.

"Yeah. Gotta get my thoughts together, ya know. Gotta see what my characters want to say to me."

CJ hadn't really gotten into writing fiction, so she found it interesting that Layla talked about her characters as though they were real people. Ms. Layla read her confusion.

"I just mean I gotta get the characters together in my head before I start putting them down on paper."

"Oh."

Ms. Layla pushed back her chair, walked over to the sink and turned on the faucet to rinse her plate. With her back still turned, she asked CJ an astonishing question.

"Who are you running from, sweetie?"

"Excuse me?"

She repeated the question. "Who are you running from?"

CJ rolled her eyes. She was so over complete strangers pretending to know her.

"Why do you say I'm running? And from what?"

Ms. Layla turned off the faucet and turned toward CJ. Her face could only be described as serenely distant. As though she was looking afar even as she peered closely.

"I've been writing a long time and living a long time. I've seen a lot."

CJ's guard went up immediately.

"So what's that mean?"

Ms. Layla chuckled.

"I love it. You're fierce, honey. A lot like me when I was your age."

CJ felt her temperature rise.

"I've heard that hundreds of times in my life and it usually ends up being as far away from the truth as I am from home."

CJ was hollow inside. Completely void of anything that even remotely resembled emotion. Ms. Layla's words could only fall on deaf ears that evening.

"Look, I'm sure you are a good woman and have good intentions, but you don't know me."

The woman didn't appear to be startled or surprised by the sharpness of CJ's words and yet she didn't intend on necessarily acknowledging them as true.

CJ continued. "We've been here all of a couple of weeks and you're claiming some kind of intimate knowledge of me. That's bull…"

Ms. Layla quickly raised her hand, stopping CJ from cursing.

She then smiled and sat back down just as CJ stood up. The younger woman was not interested in some cozy conversation with some pseudo-mother like figure. There'd be no more of her getting her hopes up only to have relationships fail her. CJ had finally become comfortable with being on her own and wanted it to stay that way. While she felt bad for disrespecting her roommate, she felt she had to make her point clear.

Ms. Layla, still smiling serenely, said, "I want to tell you something one day. I think it might help you."

CJ said, "And what makes you think I'll listen to you?"

"When you're ready, you'll listen."

CJ responded sarcastically, "Sure. Sure I will."

With that, CJ turned and went to her room, shutting the door a little louder than normal for emphasis.

Chapter 16

Mornings always found CJ taking the short walk from the guesthouse to the beach, journaling her thoughts, and making friends with the many different species of birds that flew along the coast and made their home in the rainforest. The only exception about this day was that she'd awakened two hours earlier than usual. Journal in hand, CJ stepped out from the mass of trees and vegetation and onto the expanse of white sand. Her heart stopped at what she saw before her. Sitting on *her* rock, the rock that where she'd perch and watch the rolling waves of the ocean, was Rev. Noah with his hands stretched high in the air and his mouth moving rapidly. Unsure of what to do, CJ walked further down the beach and found a place she'd hoped was out of the preacher's line of sight. She sat on an unfamiliar and less comfortable rock and focused her attention on the beautiful black bird with a reddish-orange beak that flew fearlessly in front of her. Writing for about five minutes, she decided to think of an appropriate metaphor to describe herself in relation to the bird whose feathers shone glossy in the morning sun. She couldn't think of one.

"Red-billed Curassow."

The voice came from behind her. She didn't have to turn around to know whose it was. She remained silent.

"I don't think I've ever seen one flying alone. They usually fly in pairs or groups."

Well, there was her metaphor. CJ wrote a little bit more in her journal ignoring the very manly presence behind her.

Rev. Noah walked in front of CJ and sat on the rock across from her. She looked up into his eyes and finally spoke.

"I didn't know you were an expert on birds."

"I'm not. Just some. The most beautiful ones."

CJ looked down again. She was nervous and didn't know why. There was something different about him this morning. Strange, even. Unlike the fire and brimstone preacher she'd seen the day before, he seemed, well, normal. Normal and incredibly handsome. She asked the obvious.

"You pray out here?"

"Yes."

He played along.

"You write out here?"

"Yes."

Awkwardly, CJ stood up quickly.

"Well, it was good seeing you again."

Why am I acting so corny?

"Let me walk you back."

It was then that she wanted to assert herself. Say that she could get back to the guesthouse on her own. Tell him to go back and pray some more and leave her alone. But the words would not come. It was like her will was being held hostage and the ransom was her complete compliance.

"Okay."

They walked silently at first, but then began talking about his ministry. She was fascinated by his story of growing up in Compton, California and going to jail for assault and robbery. She felt admiration take root as he shared with her how he'd changed his life, gone to seminary, and began doing missionary work. She kept telling herself she wasn't in Brazil to get caught up with some random man, especially a preacher. She'd left that drama in Chicago. But the more they talked, the more she felt herself being drawn in. The thought crossed her mind that maybe she should just have some fun. Release her heart from the bondage that love had been to her for most of her life. It wasn't like she was going to fall in love. *Especially* with a preacher. She didn't even know if she was a believer anymore, so she knew that wasn't going to work. But at least she could enjoy his company.

"I know your life is devoted to helping the people here, but what do you do for fun?"

Noah laughed.

"Fun? What's that?"

"I figured you'd say that."

CJ chalked up her plan.

"But..."

They looked at each other. Him, with purpose. Her, with hope.

She repeated after him, "But?"

"Well, there *is* the Salvador Summer Festival coming up."

She'd heard about it from Pedro, her Spanish-speaking, never-there or always-asleep housemate. He knew more about the goings on in Brazil than about the script he was supposed to be writing there.

"Yeah?" CJ played coy.

"Yeah."

About a hundred feet from her guesthouse, the two paused. She wasn't about to ask him out. That was not her thing in America or Brazil.

"Wow. It's been a long time since I've done this," Noah said.

"Done what?"

"Asked someone out."

"Oh, is that what you're doing?"

"I guess so."

CJ stared blankly at him.

"Yes, I am."

Maybe she could have a little fun after all, she thought. There was nobody here to tell her not to do it, to give her unasked for advice about not knowing anything about him or distracting the "man of God", or to guilt her into loving them because they've known each other forever. It was just her, making her own decision, and planning to show the preacher man a good time.

"Well, if you're asking then, Reverend, I'm saying yes." Noah grinned. He didn't think it would be this easy.

"I guess I'll see you next week then. The first show starts at 5pm. Take care, beautiful sister."

CJ warmed at being called beautiful. "I'll be ready. Goodbye."

On that note, they parted ways.

Noah responded under his breath.

"I hope you are, sister. I hope you are."

***

CJ came in from the beach and was greeted by the irresistible scent of breakfast cooking on the small kitchen stove. She looked over to find Miss Layla sautéing crab and beating eggs. Eating seafood in every meal, including breakfast, was common in Bahia. The closest CJ had come to having seafood for breakfast was salmon cakes at the Original Pancake House in Chicago, so she had to admit that Ms. Layla's crab omelet and fluffy pancakes drizzled with delicious sugarcane syrup smelled awfully good. Her stomach churned as the woman hummed an old Gospel tune that CJ recognized.

CJ made her presence known by intentionally bumping into a chair.

Sensing CJ standing there all along, Layla looked up just to satisfy the young woman. "Come on over here child and get something to eat."

CJ sighed with relief. After her rudeness the night before, she wasn't sure if she was welcome to any more meals. At least the kind Ms. Layla cooked. She pulled out a chair and sat down.

"I don't think Mr. Movieman is going to wake up until well after two o'clock."

CJ laughed at Layla's nickname for Pedro.

"Nah, Pedro is definitely a night owl."

Once Ms. Layla sat down, CJ dived into her plate only to stop just as quickly when she noticed the woman saying her grace. Shame, if only briefly, filled her.

For the rest of the meal, the two stayed clear of any deep conversations like the night before and just enjoyed chit chatting about writing and Brazil. Wanting to know more about Ms. Layla's former writing career, CJ asked her why she'd stopped and now was getting back into writing again.

"God had to get me right with him."

CJ, in between bites, waited for more. Ms. Layla remained silent.

Hmph! So when the tables are turned and it's time for her to start talking about her life, she gets all cryptic!

CJ probed more.

"So, you're into church and stuff?"

"No, not church. God. And Jesus."

Ms. Layla gazed at CJ knowingly. "Aren't you?"

"I used to be. But I gave it up."

"Well good thing He didn't give up on you."

Oh no, we are not going to do this again.

CJ stood up, thanked Ms. Layla for the meal, and left the room.

Chapter 17

The pile of unopened letters sitting on the tiny desk in her bedroom stared back at CJ accusingly. A few were from her godmother. Two were from Kara. Ten were from Jonathan. None had been read. It wasn't that she didn't want to read them. She just couldn't. She told herself she wanted to explore her hurt and her pain in her own way, and she wouldn't be able to do that if their voices became louder than hers through their correspondence. Plus, CJ assumed she knew what they all said. *We still love you. It's not your fault. Jesus loves you.* Not bad things by themselves, but not anything she wanted to hear, either.

And then there is Jonathan. In his case, CJ didn't necessarily assume she knew what he had written. It was more like she was scared. If it was *I love you*, then she was scared. If it was, *I made a mistake and I don't love you*, she was scared. Either way, she wasn't going to escape the sick feeling that would come over her no matter what words he used.

Nevertheless, after three months in Brazil, she did finally gather the courage to read the most recent arrival, another letter from Jonathan. In hindsight, maybe she should have read the older letter first, in order to gain some context, but CJ's logic was a little different. She read the latest letter first because if he was still writing her after three months without any response, then maybe, just maybe, the "worst" of what he needed to say was over. Unfortunately, that wasn't the case.

Dear Cris,

I must be crazy. Everyday my heart races when I pick up the mail because everyday I hope and pray there will be a letter from my best friend buried somewhere in the stack of bills. Maybe not even a letter. Maybe just a postcard. Anything would have been so much better than nothing. And yet, that's what I've gotten…nothing. I even made a fool of myself with your program coordinator. A couple of weeks ago, I called and demanded she find out if you were okay, implying you could be dead in the rainforest and nobody would know it. How embarrassing it was to hear you'd sent her an update just the day before.

So, I've made some decisions about us. About me. As I've told you repeatedly in my other letters, I love you deeply and fully and more than anybody except God and my mother. I always have. But I know I can't stand by and wait for you to love me back in the same way. Truthfully, I would have been willing to spend the rest of my life helping you heal from all you've been through, but I can only do that if you let me. And it is painfully clear that you won't. So, I've chosen to let you go. As hard as that is, I have to do it. It is the only way I'm going to not go insane.

I still wish for you nothing but joy, peace and God's greatest blessings.

Love,
The Jonnie you once called Friend

P.S. I ran into Jordyn at another conference a few weeks ago and I think I'm going to give it another shot. Despite what she did to me, I think…no, I know… my heart is much safer with her.

CJ's hands shook almost violently as tears poured out of her eyes. Jonathan was more than just a childhood friend. He had been with her through so many of her darkest hours and it was his love and prayers that comforted and soothed her. CJ closed her eyes and allowed a timeline of pictures to flash through her mind. Jonathan at six with his scrawny body, big head and even bigger smile. Jonathan at twelve, having grown somewhat into his head, and still flashing that diamond smile. By the time he was sixteen, he'd added piercing mahogany-in-the-sunlight eyes to his arsenal of attractiveness. And then, of course, there was the man. Strong in so many ways.

Maybe it's for the best, CJ thought as she wiped away her tears. Everyone else that mattered to her was gone in some way or another. As hurtful as it was, she also felt weirdly unbound. There was no one left to love her and no one left for her to love. Since her emotions were naked and bare for the first time in a long time, she would use it to fuel her writing. She'd also take more risks with her life. Returning the letter back to the envelope, CJ determined she would read the rest of them on the flight back to Chicago. To her, the worst had been said and so, deciding to roll the dice for a change, she headed to the one place where she knew her newfound risk-taking would be welcomed.

***

It had been nearly six weeks since CJ had last seen Rev. Noah or attended any of his services. The last time they'd spent time together was during the Summer Music Festival. It wasn't so much that something had gone wrong during their date or that they didn't have a good time together. It was more about his schedule and how the ministry kept him traveling up and down the South American coast. Plus, if she was honest, CJ would have to admit she'd take the company of just plain ole' Noah, the one who danced the samba in the streets and whose very movements made her sweat over the preaching, healing, tongue-talking Reverend any day. The time they did spend together was not only fun, but as CJ described it...magical. It gave her an opportunity to enjoy the company of a man without there being any past to reckon with or any subtext to their conversation. However, now that CJ's perspective had changed a bit after receiving the "Dear Jane" letter from Jonathan, she finally realized she desired subtext in the worst way. She knew the only way she would be able to get that kind of attention would be to position herself in such a way he'd have to truly be divine to ignore her.

CJ entered the back of the tent about a half hour after the start of the service and sat in the chair nearest the center aisle in the last row. She wasn't surprised by the looks of the female elders who ushered her in. Dressed in a red, wrap dress that hugged every bit of her South side of Chicago curves, she meant to draw attention to herself. In fact, as she sat down, she crossed her legs knowing full well that all of the beach walking she'd done over the last few months resulted in the newly defined calf muscles that seemed to speak for themselves. Upon sitting, CJ looked up just in time for her eyes to meet his. She thought she saw something slightly more than recognition. Maybe it was a spark of interest hidden carefully behind the veil of religious decorum. Either way, it was all the reassurance she needed.

The service ended predictably with a long line of people waiting for prayer. CJ was patient, though. She sat and waited until the last person thanked the preacher for delivering a *mighty* word. She waited because she was confident the two red-brown brothers would soon come for her, bringing her to the second tent where Rev. Noah kept his things. After ten minutes or so, her prediction came true as the brothers called her to the back tent. She stood up, readjusted her dress and walked to the other tent under the watchful eyes of Noah's men. As she pulled the entryway curtains back, she was greeted by Noah's smile. Looking at the two brothers who'd followed her in, he communicated his wishes without saying a word. Knowingly, they turned and exited quickly. Following their lead, the young, Jamaican-Chinese nurse who'd brought in water and juice, also left the room.

The religious veil that covered his eyes fell completely and entirely as he took in the beautiful woman in front of him.

"How are you?" He said.

"Lonely." CJ wasted no time.

His face registered his shock at her boldness and then just as quickly transformed into approval. He moved closer to her.

"You know, I usually never allow myself to be alone in a room with a woman, especially after preaching."

"So why am I here?"

Noah chuckled out loud and continued to fill the two feet of space between them. "I've been asking myself that same question, dear."

CJ liked trading wits with the minister and decided to test him.

"Shouldn't you be asking God?"

Noah's smile vanished and he stopped walking toward her. Immediately, CJ regretted her statement.

"I'm sorry. I shouldn't have said that."

Noah said nothing at first. He just looked at CJ as though he were reading her. CJ grew nervous under his stare, but enjoyed being the book he was checking out. After searching her eyes for what seemed like eternity, Noah took the liberty to roam her body openly. CJ felt woozy as though she was being hypnotized by his gaze. So much so that she had to steady herself by gripping the folding chair in front of her.

"Can I walk you back," Noah asked.

"Of course."

He grabbed his bags and escorted her out of the tent. CJ felt liberated by the stares of those who watched them leave the grounds knowing they'd already begun to speculate about the preacher and the woman in the red dress.

After ten minutes of walking in silence, Noah stopped and turned to CJ.

"I would like for you to come work for me."

CJ laughed a little too loudly. Noah didn't even smile.

"Oh. You're serious?"

"Yes. I would like for you to come volunteer at the ministry. You're gifted. Why is that funny?"

CJ decided to seize the opportunity and stepped seductively to Noah, this time making sure there was no room left between them.

"And what would you like for me to do for you, uh, I mean, the ministry?"

Noah took one step back. CJ wasn't surprised at his reaction.

"We have a newsletter..."

"...but I don't speak Portuguese or Spanish," CJ interrupted.

"You don't have to. We have translators. I need you..."

"You need me, Reverend?"

Noah smiled.

"The ministry needs you to help with the format, structure and the content. Since you worked at a magazine, I thought..."

CJ cut him off again. "..you thought you could *use* me, I mean, my expertise."

Noah paused and thought about the implications of what she was saying.

"Yes, in a way, I guess you're right."

CJ immediately thought about her father and the classic Bill Withers song he used to play all the time.

I wanna spread the news that if it feels this good getting used, then you just keep on using me, until you use me up.

Noah noticed CJ's mind drifted in that moment, but didn't comment on it. It only added to his interest in her. They continued walking down the road.

"So will you help?"

"Yes, but..."

Noah reached for CJ's hand and held it as they walked. His touch filled her with warmth.

"...I don't even know if I believe anymore."

"Believe?"

"Yes, believe. I mean, I know God exists. But I don't feel the same way about Him that I used to. I don't know if I can trust Him like I used to. That's what I mean by believe. I'm sure you want someone with a faith stronger than that."

CJ stopped and looked at Noah hopefully as she realized her statement's double meaning.

"It's okay, beautiful sister." He gently touched her cheek and she trembled.

They continued walking in silence until they arrived at the guesthouse. CJ was grateful for him walking her back and told him as much. Lately, she'd been seeing shadows in the trees and it frightened her. Knowing the rainforest was filled with lurking creatures, she tried her best to ignore them when walking by herself at dusk or afterwards.

Noah sensed her fear and, speaking in a soft comforting tone, he responded to her earlier statement.

"You know, CJ, even if you don't believe in what I preach, at least not so much, please know you can believe in me."

That was comforting to CJ, even if it did feel a bit pretentious. Noah took CJ's hand, the one he was still holding, and kissed her softly on the inside of her palm, while never taking his eyes off her face. She moved closer to the preacher until the air became thick with heat and she was nose to nose with him. CJ kissed him. Gently at first then deeper, until they were both lost in the moment. Noah held CJ's face in his hands, his body responding to the thin silk of her dress.

After a few minutes, he hesitantly pulls away from her and CJ sensed his conflict.

"I'm sorry," she said as she lowered her head.

"Don't be."

Noah took her chin between his index and thumb fingers and lifted her face toward him.

"God is the author of love."

The shadows CJ saw just beyond Noah's shoulder dimmed greatly in the light that shone brightly from his eyes. Although she tried her best to hold her emotions at bay and the Spirit she'd grown accustomed to ignoring had become deafeningly still, her heart leaped at the thought of being able to love and trust again. Her body, however, responded in another manner altogether. She felt the rumble of nausea take over.

160

Noah turned away and headed back out to the trail that lead to the main road.

"I'll see you soon?"

The discomfort in CJ's stomach became more violent. "Yes," she said hurriedly.

As she watched him disappear behind the trees, CJ frantically pulled out her keys, opened the door, and, holding her stomach in one hand and covering her mouth with the other, rushed into bathroom.

Chapter 18

After CJ calmed the sudden turbulence of her stomach, she washed up and headed toward the main room where Ms. Layla was sitting in her favorite spot at the kitchen table eating a bowl of fruit and writing on a notepad. CJ wondered if she was sitting there the whole time, but did not ask.

Looking up from her writing, Layla stared at the young woman who was moving nervously about the kitchen trying to ignore her. She smiled.

"Be careful."

CJ stopped what she was doing, which was basically nothing, and sat down in the chair across from Layla.

"What do you mean?"

"Everything is not what it seems with him."

CJ didn't bother to pretend she didn't know who the woman was talking about. She'd grown tired of Layla's constant commentary on her life and didn't feel like she needed to hide anything from someone who she considered to be a bitter, washed up writer with nothing else better to do. Her anger was evident in her face and tone.

"You don't know that!"

Layla responded to CJ's irritation with her signature calm and composed voice, "Oh, but I do. I do know that."

CJ stood up and considered leaving only stopping to realize darkness had completely enveloped the trail leading to the road and to the beach. *Can't deal with the shadows.* She turned and headed toward her bedroom.

"You should talk about what happened at home." Layla's words pierced CJ's soul. She turned around and tried unsuccessfully to remind herself that this woman didn't know anything about her.

"What are you talking about NOW, *Miss* Layla?"

Layla got up from the table and walked over to CJ.

"Sweetie, don't be scared. I'm not trying to be spooky or anything. I just know a runner when I see one…in the spirit and in the natural."

Although she rolled her eyes, CJ could feel it. Tears, real drops of liquid pain, were trying to take her pride hostage. But she wouldn't allow it. She would not break. Although she had to admit she was intrigued by the woman's words, she was still too consumed by her own selfishness to allow any of it to penetrate her too deeply.

This should be interesting. Good fodder for my writing. Maybe I can create a character just like her. Any rationalization was easier for CJ than hearing the truth.

"Walk with me," Layla said as she pointed to the door.

CJ hesitated.

"There is nothing to be afraid of that you haven't already seen."

Layla led CJ to the door.

"It's too dark. We can talk right here."

"Come on, hon. Don't worry. I got you covered."

As they walked the short distance to the beach, CJ noticed the shadows she normally saw were gone. No unseen animals were lying in wait behind the fog and trees as they were when she ventured out at night. The two women walked a little further onto the beach until they found a wooden bench and, for a few moments, sat and watched the tide come in. The moon was bright over the Atlantic Ocean as an unfamiliar peacefulness settled around CJ.

She stared hard in the darkness at the faint line of the long-gone horizon. A memory seized her. This time it was of her and Jonathan sitting on Chicago's Navy Pier and watching

163

the waters of Lake Michigan. A tear found its freedom and slid down her cheek.

Layla spoke softly as her eyes reached for the stars above them.

"Crystal, there *is* such a thing as heaven. There is such a thing as a natural realm and a spiritual realm."

She didn't know why, but Layla's words made CJ think about her father and her mother. She imagined them finding each other again, this time in heaven. She smiled to herself and then quickly remembered she was supposed to not care.

"And sometimes the natural realm and the spiritual realm are quite parallel in activity. What do you think about that?"

"There was once a time where I wouldn't have questioned what you're saying. But now… I just don't know."

Layla continued. "Do you see that ocean?"

"Yes."

"You believe it exists, right?"

"Yes."

"What about the sand?"

"What about it?"

"Do you believe it exists?"

CJ was exasperated. "Of course, I do. It's right there! Come on, Ms. Layla, where are you going with this?"

"Just humor an old woman, okay?"

A few more minutes passed between them before Layla spoke again.

"Do you believe there are spiritual beings all around us?"

CJ fell silent. She recalled how her Aunt Kara used to always talk about seeing and walking in the spirit, and how there were angelic beings and demonic beings around us. But CJ thought it all sounded too mystic for her. It felt too hokey. Right now, it was hard enough for her to believe in God, the Devil and Jesus. Plus, thinking about this stuff caused her to think about her recent past and she just couldn't bring herself to do that yet.

Layla didn't expect an answer from CJ. She was familiar with how the young woman was feeling.

"Do you hear from God, CJ?"

CJ felt her emotions shift. She recalled a time when she did.

Ms. Layla continued. "You ask me, 'How do I know you're running from something' and 'How do I know that man is not what he seems'?"

"Yes. How do you know that?"

"All I can say is that, through my prayers, I've seen you in the spirit. When you hear from God clearly, He will show you things. Just as sure as I see you right now, sitting next to me, I've seen..." Layla shook her head, which sparked CJ's curiosity.

"Yeah? What did you see?"

Layla sensed the young woman wasn't ready to hear it all, but decided to dig a little deeper.

"...well, I saw you running."

"Running." *Okay, lady, that's convenient. You could have come up with something better than that lame metaphor.*

"Yes, running. It seemed like you were being chased."

"Chased? By who?"

Layla pondered the question before speaking.

"By yourself. By God. By..."

"Wait a minute!" CJ interrupted. "I'm confused."

"I know. It is quite confusing."

"You saw me being chased by myself *and* by God?"

"Yes, and you were also being chased by..."

"No, no, no, no, no!"

CJ's tears flowed freely now. "Why would God be chasing me? Better yet. Why would I be chasing myself?"

This woman is crazy. I think.

"How do you know I was being chased? Maybe I was running away."

"Perhaps." Layla didn't want to overwhelm her, but CJ continued to press her.

"Tell me more."

165

Layla smiled. "Let's start with the first thing. Running from yourself. Can you imagine what that looks like?"

"Uh, actually, no."

"Well imagine it in the natural realm and I can assure you it looks even crazier in the spiritual."

CJ pictured herself in duplicate. In her mind's eye, she saw herself chasing herself. *Yeah, that does look strange.*

"When you run away from yourself, you are literally running in circles. You are making a futile attempt to get away from something that is very much a part of you. You run and then you look up and the thing you were running away from is still there. It is truly the breeding ground for insanity."

"So maybe I'm crazy then," CJ said sarcastically. "I'm not saying I believe what you're saying, but if it's true, then my being crazy makes sense. It explains why my life has been the way it is and why I have had to endure so much loss."

"No, baby. You're not crazy. That would be entirely too easy."

Layla felt CJ's bewilderment.

"I know you must have experienced some great pains in your life. The wounds look to be so fresh."

"Wounds? Is that something else you see in the…" CJ hesitated and then sarcastically raised her fingers to make air quotes. "…spiritual realm?"

"As a matter of fact, it is."

CJ sighed.

"Don't be weary, love. Remember I said God is chasing you, too."

"Now *that* I really don't understand."

"I believe you do. You remember what it felt like to hear him, don't you?"

CJ didn't answer.

"You remember when His Holy Spirit would comfort you, right?"

CJ still didn't respond. Layla leaned over and whispered into CJ's ear.

"Did you think He would let you go without a fight?"

CJ's face and hands were drenched with tears at this point, even though she maintained a very detached and despondent expression. "Who else," she said.

Layla was startled. "Excuse me?"

"Before I cut you off, you were going to tell me who else you saw chasing me."

The old woman closed her eyes. She needed guidance on this one.

"Listen. Just know if what is going on in the natural is any indication of what is happening in the spiritual realm, then there is a great war going on over you."

"A war?"

"Yes."

"What kind of war?"

"In general? A war between good and evil."

Okay, now I'm in the middle of a Star Wars movie. Geesh!

"And I'm not talking about something you'd see in a movie either."

Now CJ was officially freaked out.

"Okay. So is that why you said to be careful about Rev. Noah?"

It was Layla's turn to be silent.

"Is he the evil that's going to 'get' me?"

"No, he's just a man. It's bigger than him."

"Right! He *is* just a man. A very fine man who likes me and is not afraid to show it. So, if he is the one that's chasing me, then you better believe I'm going to stop and let him catch me."

Layla shook her head and stood up, signaling it was time for them to make their way back to the guesthouse.

As they walked back to the house, CJ noticed the shadows had returned. Layla didn't seem to notice or be frightened by them, so she reached out and held on to the woman's arm.

When they were about ten feet away from the door, CJ turned to Layla and said, "A war, huh?"

Layla smiled.

In a way, I guess that makes sense.

"Well, if what you saw is true and what I know is true, then you're probably right." The faint whisper of CJ's spirit, a spirit that had been buried beneath the sediment of her loss, pain, and need for unconditional love, had already confirmed it so.

***

Jonathan pulled from his pocket the delivery confirmation ticket from the post office. It was done. She'd received the letter and still, no response. He didn't know what else to do. He looked over at Jordyn who'd fallen asleep on the couch watching a movie. He hated the fact he was using her now as she'd used him before. It wasn't that he didn't like her. He liked her very much. She was beautiful, even as she slept. She was a brilliant woman who could open many doors for him in his career. But none of that mattered to him because his heart just wasn't in it. Given the circumstances, Jonathan had reconciled that the woman he loved with every fiber of his being would probably not be the woman he married. Jordyn was like a comfortable and familiar blanket. In spite of what she did in the past, at least he always knew where he stood with her. Plus, while his heart was wandering the streets of Brazil, it...she...was still very much broken and he wasn't strong enough to put it or her back together again. That was a job for the potter Himself. Jonathan walked into the guest bedroom and kneeled down along the side of the bed.

"Father, I know I don't deserve to speak with you right now, but thank you for your grace and mercy. I know you answer prayer, even if the answer is not always what we'd like hear. I've prayed so much for my own satisfaction in this situation instead of surrendering to your will and for that, I ask for forgiveness. But this time, Lord, I don't come to you for me and what I want. I come to you for her. I feel her soul crying out to me even though she's so very far away, Lord. I don't know what is happening to her, but I know you are a deliverer. Crystal Germaine, in spite of her pain, is your daughter and you said you would never leave her or forsake her. Please remember your Word. Cover her, Lord. Protect her. From the seen and unseen. In Jesus' name, Amen."

168

Jonathan's face was wet with tears when he finished. He took his right hand and wiped his sadness away with one stroke. He felt a peace he couldn't explain and that soothed him a bit. After being squeezed shut during his prayer, his eyes began adjusting to the light in the room, unfortunately in just enough time to meet the shocked face of Jordyn who was standing in the doorway of the room. She'd awakened when she'd heard his voice and walked in on him as he was praying. Her face was draped with frustration as she stared back at her boyfriend with eyes that offered both accusation and sympathy. Without saying a word, she walked back into the next room. It was clear she understood Jonathan would never apologize for praying for CJ nor did she feel right asking him to do so.

Jonathan stood up and went into the bathroom to take a shower. He was unwilling and unable to explain to Jordyn his feelings for CJ, and Jordyn wasn't sure she wanted to know. They both settled for silence.

Chapter 19

The morning after her encounter with Layla, CJ stayed in bed. It was the first time she did not make the trek out to the beach to write. As a matter of fact, she hadn't really written much at all in the past weeks. She heard Layla's words in her head clearly and repeatedly, so she knew going back to a place she first heard them would only make them louder and more persistent.

She'd been read. Not in the normal sistergirl way she was used to, though. This was different. Layla *really* read her. It was like she'd been some secret agent voyeur, peeking into her life and intentionally pressing up against all of CJ's tender places. That's a fifty-cent way of saying she knew things she wasn't supposed to know. CJ wanted to brush it off by saying the woman spoke in generalities, but in her heart, she knew better. Too bad knowing better doesn't always mean doing better.

CJ decided to spend the rest of her time in Brazil writing, working on Rev. Noah's newsletter and staying as far away from Ms. Layla as one can from someone who lived in the same house. She was more than halfway through the fellowship, so while she would have to tolerate the woman's loud praying and singing, and yes, would probably have to give up the wonderful meals she cooked, at the end of the day, it would all be worth it if she could avoid having anymore deep conversations or taking anymore late-night walks to the beach.

***

She couldn't explain it, but working with Rev. Noah's ministry felt different from the work she'd done at her church in Chicago. At the church of her youth, she always felt like she was up close and personal with God and that everything she did was for Him. It wasn't like that with Rev. Noah's ministry. In fact, the only person she felt up close and personal with was Rev. Noah, and that was fine with her.

CJ was surprised to find out the business of the ministry was not held in the tents where services were held. Those were for community gatherings only. Administrative business was conducted in a small conference room at a luxury hotel on the other side of Salvador. Near the bay side of the peninsula. This was a part of the city that CJ hadn't spent much of her time. There was a growing tourist industry and many wealthy, foreign investors were building resorts and hotels on both the bay side and the ocean side. While CJ found the more rural areas and the beaches much more conducive to her purpose, but she couldn't help but to be curious about the city now that she was attending one of Rev. Noah's meetings.

During the staff meeting, CJ quickly surveyed the other members of the ministry team. The red-brown brothers, whose names she finally learned were Gabriel and Lucas, sat on either side of the preacher. The Jamaican-Chinese woman with thick, night-black hair and dark, slanted eyes sat across from CJ. Three other men, locals she assumed, sat at the opposite end of the long table and to CJ's right sat a British woman with tiny, mousy lips and too-long dirty blond hair.

Boy, isn't this a strange looking bunch!

Jumping right into the meeting, Rev. Noah began with his review of the content for the newsletter. CJ thought she'd done a good a job of capturing the services offered by the ministry as well as the other outreach efforts being carried on across the state, country and continent. Everyone in the room seemed to be holding their breath, but she felt confident about

171

her work and smiled as Rev. Noah went through each section silently.

Looking up from the papers in front of him, the preacher looked around the room, finally allowing his eyes to reach CJ, who continued to smile until she looked closer at his face. His eyes were dead. No emotion. No flicker of recognition. CJ thought maybe she'd messed up and began to worry as she waited for his response.

Still staring at CJ, along with everyone else now, he finally spoke.

"Good job, Crystal."

That was it. Rev. Noah moved on to the next item on his agenda, an upcoming evangelistic event, which he began to discuss with one of the local men. To say she felt slighted would be an understatement. It wasn't as though she expected some great praise, but she didn't expect it to be cast aside as though her task was a meaningless one. While sitting at the table, CJ's mind flashed back to her experiences with her college boyfriend, Ike. She'd spent much of their relationship seeking his approval and this one simple diss felt awfully close to that familiar feeling of rejection she'd felt back then.

Why do I care?

Why did she care? In her mind, she told herself she had no intentions of pursuing a relationship with the reverend. Yes, he was fine. Yes, there was something unexplainable that drew her to him.

But I'm just a writer on a fellowship in Brazil who decided to spend the last couple of months helping a local ministry. Why should I care whether he accepts me or not?

Because she always had. She knew it even if she never admitted. Her stuff, past stuff, stuff she thought she'd buried with her father, was showing up again, and this time without any provocation from an old woman with skin the color of brown leather and supernatural sight. CJ decided she would leave this meeting, but before doing so decided to finally tune in to the conversation that Rev. Noah was having with one of the staffers.

"What do you mean you couldn't get the venue," Rev. Noah said between gritted teeth.

The man just sat there wide-eyed as the preacher continued to question him.

"Don't you think you need to do a better job at what I tell you to do or maybe this isn't the place for you?"

CJ was stunned at the harshness of Noah's tone. The man's head dropped to his chest.

"I tried, Father. I told them it was for you, but they said someone had booked that day a year in advance and had put a sizeable deposit down."

Did he just say Father?

Rev. Noah's shoulders straightened and something other than Godliness stole the brightness from his eyes.

"I don't care if they booked it fifteen years ago. I WANT THAT SPACE." Rev. Noah lowered the volume of his voice when he noticed the pure shock that crossed CJ's face.

In something just a little louder than a whisper he said, "I want that space, Pedro, and you are going to get it for me..."

He paused, looking around the table at the other staffers to make sure they caught his message.

"...or else."

The man shook noticeably as he fumbled with his papers and stood up.

"Y-y-yes. Yesss, s-s-s-ir. I will do that."

He practically ran out of the room.

CJ was done. She'd seen plenty of people pull a Jekyl and Hyde before, but this was unbelievable. The man in that conference room couldn't have been the man who'd held her hand as they walked to her guesthouse; the man who'd danced the samba in the streets during the music festival; the man who'd kissed her so sweetly and so gently. Although she wasn't feeling God right now, she still had the expectation that those who professed to be his mouthpiece were to uphold his standards of how to treat people.

Maybe Ms. Layla was right.

CJ finally pushed back from the table, stood and picked up her bag to leave. Everyone else at the table watched her as she readied herself to make a quick and permanent exit. Rev. Noah adjourned the meeting hastily and without once removing his eyes from CJ. She saw him staring at her, but felt a greater pull to leave without entertaining any explanations. The nurse and the British woman were the first to leave, followed by the two remaining local men. Finally, after being given the nod, the red-brown brothers left the room. CJ walked toward the door intending to follow right behind them.

"Sister Crystal."

CJ ignored him.

"Crystal." This time he raised his voice a bit.

CJ turned toward him. "For the record, speaking louder will not make me respond any faster. I am not one of your people."

CJ twisted her body abruptly to leave and then just as quickly turned back to face him again.

"Or maybe I should say, I'm not one of your children, *Father*."

In three long strides, Noah was standing in front of her. CJ's skin crawled with fear until she looked up and into his eyes. The softness had returned.

"I'm so sorry."

CJ couldn't give in. Not yet, anyway.

"Sorry for what? Sorry that you spoke to that poor man that way or sorry I saw you do it."

"Both."

"Hmph!"

Noah sighed. CJ needed more than an apology. Noah was willing to oblige her.

He sat down on the sofa that was positioned along the wall nearest the door. He invited CJ to sit next to him and against the movement of her spirit, as faint as it was, she sat.

"I'm just a man, Sister."

Unexpectedly, Noah began to sob. Softly at first, then louder. Giant tears seemed to rush down the chiseled darkness

174

of his face. For the second time that day, CJ was stunned. Her bag was still hanging from her arm, so she put it down on the floor beside the couch. She took it all in. His tears. The sudden smallness of a larger-than-life man. The jagged movements of his shoulders as he cried.

"This. Is. Difficult." He said.

"I didn't want to be mean to him. But, I'm human."

CJ didn't buy his reasoning, but kept her voice gentle. "But that's not an excuse to treat people that way."

"I know." Noah paused and looked up at her. "It's just that these people, they put me up on a pedestal. I can never be angry. I can never be sad. I can never be tired. I can never be selfish."

CJ noticed Noah was working himself up again and she, unaware of her own movements, shifted over a couple of inches toward him.

"But guess what? I do get angry. I do get sad. I am tired. And yes, sometimes, I'm selfish. How does that change what I do here?" He didn't wait for CJ to respond. In fact, if she didn't already know they were the only ones in the room, she would have thought he was speaking to someone else.

"Right! It doesn't. But these people are so…so….needy. They don't want anything less than what is in that pulpit. If they only knew…"

Noah stopped himself.

She couldn't help but to feel something. Her heart grew more connected to him with each word he spoke. CJ didn't think she needed some supernatural sight to see what he was going through and she didn't think Ms. Layla had any either. At least when it came to this man. It was true that, in some ways, she pitied him. But her pity, mixed with his seemingly genuine vulnerability, created a cocktail of attraction she couldn't fight, if she wanted to.

Noah twisted his body in order to face CJ. The tears were gone from his eyes and left behind was flaming desire. Immediately affected by the passion in his gaze, CJ's eyes mirrored his, making their own request. He spoke first.

"I know God has something for you, but I just haven't been released to tell you yet."

A part of CJ clearly warned her to not be sucked in by the intensity of the moment. She couldn't help but to hear Ms. Layla's voice in her head. *Everything about him is not what it seems.* But there was another part of her that Noah had been able to reach more precisely with his words. The part that desperately wanted to know what God had for her, particularly since everything she thought she'd had was gone. She couldn't help but to be intrigued by the idea that a man like this, one who made parts of her body she never knew existed come alive, could actually know.

"Why can't you tell me?"

"Because it's not time yet."

CJ dropped her head.

"But I will. I promise, you'll know soon."

He lifted CJ's head with his index finger and tenderly pulled her face toward his. Their mouths met in a soft kiss that rapidly turned more insistent. A transference of need took place as she succumbed to the fruit of his lips. Pulling back, Noah stood up and picked up CJ's bag. With his other hand, he helped her off the sofa and led her out of the conference room, down the hall, and into a secluded hotel suite for which he had a key. CJ felt the nausea returning, but this time refused to allow her body to frustrate her with its mixed signals. The idea of taking a little bit of Rev. Noah's love, whether counterfeit or not, back home was very appealing in that instant. She was determined to step out into the deep and pray...well, maybe just hope...she would be able to stay afloat.

Chapter 20

CJ awakened late the next morning with her head filled with noise. The noise was actually more like voices that crowded her mind and threatened to overtake her own. Some of the voices were ones she recognized. Ms. Layla. Her father. Her Nana. Aunt Kara. Jonathan. But then there were the ones whose sound was unfamiliar, even though she felt like she'd heard them before. Each voice vied for her attention and in doing, so caused her head to throb. She opened her eyes and looked around the room realizing for the first time she was in her own bed.

How did I get here?

Having no memory of how she'd gotten back to the guesthouse, CJ searched her mind for some clue as to exactly what happened after she was so wonderfully escorted to Noah's hotel suite.

She sat up in the bed and leaned against a stack of pillows behind her. It wasn't until her body became chilled by the light breeze that came through the window screen that she realized she was completely naked. CJ pulled up the sheet and rubbed her arms and legs for warmth. That's when she noticed the strain in the muscles of her inner thighs. Rubbing her stomach next, she felt the tension in her abdomen. It felt as though she'd done a million crunches. Her eyes were finally drawn to the welts that had grown fat and red around her wrists and ankles. It was then that she remembered.

Amazing.

CJ breathed deeply. His scent was still with her. Images flashed through her mind as she laid back prostrate on the bed and stared at the ceiling. Every single one of her sexual experiences, from her unfortunate first time to her painful encounters with Ike, made her feel guilty and ashamed; as though she was condemned forever by her fornication. But this time it was different. The emptiness was still there, but the guilt and shame wasn't. In fact, she didn't feel anything at all. Correction. She did feel something. An overwhelming craving to see the man who took away her guilt and shame and spend every waking moment in his presence.

In CJ's mind, the night she shared with the reverend was truly a divine experience. He was able to take her to, what seemed like, another dimension. A place parallel to reality, but where she could forget her pain and become intoxicated by the moment. A place where she could be consumed by her own desire and not feel bad about it. He was the one, she thought. The one who could save her from the hurt.

The still, small Voice that would have normally whispered reason into her heart was undetectable and CJ was glad. That part of her was dead and gone, and she told herself it was for the best. She loved the high of what she felt the night before and in that instant, all she could think about was his eyes, his touch, his kiss and his words. In one night, she'd become addicted and just like the fiend she'd become, CJ began to plan how she would get her next hit.

***

Two weeks later, CJ had not heard from Rev. Noah. She'd tried to call his cell phone, but there was never any answer. The tent services had been moved to another location and would not return to the part of town where she stayed for two more days. She didn't know if she could last that long. Every day without contact felt like death. She didn't eat much and writing was definitely out of the question. Sleeping was even more difficult because she'd begun to have some of the most awful nightmares. Images of skeletons running towards a bright light, but breaking into a million pieces filled her nights. She felt like she was going insane.

On one of her worst days, CJ finally ventured out of her room to search the kitchen for something, anything that she could eat without vomiting. Ms. Layla was seated at the kitchen table, as usual. CJ sighed at the sight of her roommate. She knew how she must have looked to the woman. Moving quickly to the cupboards, she looked for food.

Layla closed her eyes. A tear escaped them and slid down her cheek, becoming lost in the folds beneath her chin. Each time CJ slammed a cabinet, it felt like the lash of a whip to Layla's heart. She wanted to help the girl, but she knew God's timing was always best.

CJ grabbed a box of crackers and walked back to her room. Her robe hung lifelessly from her body as she held the box close to her chest with one hand and her robe closed with the other. Layla's soft voice caught up with her.

"It's called a soul tie and unfortunately you've created a monster of one."

CJ had heard about soul ties. Her pastor back in Chicago used to tell the teenagers that when they had sex with someone, they were connected to that person forever. CJ didn't buy it, though. Even if the evidence proved otherwise, she refused to believe this was something she couldn't shake if she wanted to. She just didn't want to right now.

CJ didn't turn around to face Layla, but she did respond.

"You got it all figured out, huh?"

Layla closed her eyes again.

"God knows you, baby. He's always known you."

CJ walked back into her room and slammed the door.

After that, CJ stayed in her room. She didn't want to run into Ms. Layla again for fear of what she'd say. It was bad enough that she still had to listen to the woman's singing and praying. Layla was bold enough to even pray for CJ aloud. However, none of it was soothing anymore. It all sounded like crashing symbols, making her head pound and her heart race.

There *was* a small part of CJ that considered how she was acting and feeling to be very strange. But even then, pride kept her from asking for help.

Two more days went by and CJ had repeatedly been snatched from slumber in the middle of the night sweating and shaking with a strange combination of yearning and hatred. She didn't understand what was happening. So, for the first time in weeks, she turned to her journal.

God, I miss him. Every fiber of my being longs to see him again. To feel his arms wrapped around my waist. To taste the sweetness of his kisses. To lie next to him and admire his sleeping face. The hurt I feel is so unimaginable. Why doesn't he call or come by? Maybe this is love and I'm just not used to it yet. I've heard that sometimes love can make you run hot and then cold. That never happened to me before, but maybe it wasn't love before. Maybe this is. Yet, something still doesn't seem right. This feels so...so...different. Like some kind of spell. Like he has some kind of hold on me. I can't find any comfort or peace, which is something I need so bad right now. I feel so disconnected as though I've detached from life. Actually more than comfort, what I really need is courage.

CJ gathered up some of that courage and prepared herself to see Noah. She wanted to present herself to him as freely as she did back in the hotel room in Salvador. She would do whatever it took to feel the way she felt then. So, when the tent service returned, she decided to attend and afterwards pay the reverend a visit.

She wore the red wrap dress that had caught his attention over a month before. Only this time because of her weight loss, it hung unflatteringly loose around her hips. CJ's eyes were encased by black rings of sleeplessness and bulged with the evidence of her constant crying. Still, she had to see him. When she walked into the tent, she expected that, like before, all eyes would be on her. Surely they knew she was his woman. But no one acknowledged her. Not even the elderly women who'd ushered her in. In spite of the obvious indifference, she pressed on.

If I can only catch his eye. See that sparkle of recognition.

CJ didn't get as much as a glance from Noah. Frustrated, she stood up and began to pretend as though she was praising God. Waving her hands in the air and shouting hallelujah, CJ joined in with the others who were shouting and jumping. Again, nothing worked. Noah never looked her way.

Desperate, CJ decided to wait in the prayer line. If he couldn't see her in the audience, he'd have to see her when he laid hands on her. Her heart beat wildly in her ears as the line became shorter and she got closer to the preacher. When she made it to the front, she smiled seductively at him. He looked at her, smiled and communicated one of his silent orders to Lucas, the larger of the red-brown brothers. Lucas stood behind CJ as Noah raised his hand over her head. She was acutely aware he didn't touch her as he had the others and so she stood on her tip toes in order to make her head reach his hovering hand. However, Noah simply lifted his hand higher so she couldn't feel his touch and continued to pray.

"O, Holy One, your daughter has come here seeking something…" He began.

CJ couldn't hear what he was saying and didn't care. She was deafened by her desperation. Her only concern was letting him know he could have her; that he'd already had her. That she was willing to stay in Brazil to be with him. That she'd even call him Father if he'd just touch her once more. That is when she reached out and wrapped her arms around his neck.

Noah stood there frozen by her embrace and yet never stopping his prayer. He did not want to alarm any of the other attendees.

"Pray for our sister, everyone. Right now! Close your eyes and pray for this wretched woman."

Wretched?

When CJ heard that she wailed loudly.

Lucas quickly loosened CJ's grasp on the preacher and pulled her back. Something inside of CJ found more strength to fight off the bodyguard, but eventually failed to break free from his clutches. Lucas picked her up and took her to the smaller tent where she continued to scream until she lost most of her voice.

Fifteen minutes later, the curtain that served as a doorway to the tent opened and Noah stepped in. Behind him was a young woman CJ had never seen before. The curvaceous woman was dressed in a floor-length, A-line dress patterned with large red and white flowers; had a smooth, peanut-brown complexion and hazel-green eyes that reminded CJ of the cat that used to hang around her Nana's house. Suddenly conscious of her appearance, CJ straightened up her clothes and looked wildly back and forth between the two.

Noah turned to the woman and kissed her openly on the lips. "Misha, dear, do you mind waiting for me outside?" Misha looked at CJ, starting at her feet and ending at her tear-stained face. She smiled confidently.

"Sure thing, love."

CJ shook her head and as soon as the woman left reached out to hold Noah.

"Don't do that, Crystal," he said, moving out of the path of her embrace.

Her arms still held out to him, C.J. retorted, "What do you mean? Don't do what?"

Noah walked over to his bag and began packing it.

CJ pointed toward the entryway. "Who is she?"

He ignored her.

"Who is she, Noah?"

Noah turned to CJ. "That is no concern of yours."

"It's been almost three weeks since that night."

Noah looked over his shoulder to see if anyone was standing outside of the tent.

He then stepped closer to CJ with a menacing stance and fury written all over face. His eyes seemed to glow as he captured CJ's gaze and held it in a fierce, trance-like manner.

"You will NEVER speak of that night again!"

"But..."

Noah grabbed CJ's upper arm and pulled her close to him. She felt conflict as the lure of being so near to him

182

contrasted with the fear she felt in the pit of her stomach. She looked up at him and saw nothing she'd seen before. His eyes were black and shadowed.

"Did you hear me?" He spoke through his teeth.

"Okay." CJ replied timidly.

Whispering, she said, "But we were together. You took..."

Noah roughly let go of her arm causing her to nearly fall backwards over the chair that was just behind her. He read the confusion in her face and although he swore he'd never explain himself to a woman, he decided to make sure the knife he used to cut into her soul was firmly in place.

"I only took what you gave me. I actually thought you would've been more of a challenge. But you weren't. Yeah, I had to shed a few tears and tell a few stories, but you were no challenge at all." His laugh was sinister as he continued.

"It was like leading a horse to water."

He laughed louder.

"And man, were you thirsty, sister!"

Even as tiny explosions seemed to go off in her head, CJ still pressed him.

"Can you tell me something?"

Noah's sigh sounded strangely like relief to CJ.

"What," he said sharply.

"You said God wanted to show me something."

Noah's wicked smile returned.

"I did say that, didn't I?"

CJ folded her arms across her chest and leaned her head to one side. It was all she could do to not break into a million pieces.

"Yes. But I never found out what it was."

Noah backed up toward the entryway laughing so loudly that the sound of his voice seemed to echo.

"Oh, but you did, didn't you?"

And then he was gone. CJ rushed out of the tent only to find that when she stepped outside she was alone. Alone in more ways than the physical. Everyone, including Noah and his new diversion Misha, had left the meeting site. CJ stood in the place where just a few hours ago, people were praising and shouting to a God she'd abandoned. Rejected, humiliated and brokenhearted, she'd hit the bottom. At twilight, the American woman with the wrinkled red dress walked along the trail back to the main road. The shadows she usually saw at night seemed closer than ever.

***

The presence that seemed to be pressing behind her, frightened CJ as she walked back to the guesthouse. She tried to ignore it. She even tried talking to herself about it.

"It's all in my mind. There is nothing out there," she said aloud to herself.

And yet, the more she walked, the closer it seemed to get. Her fear would not allow her to turn around and face whatever it was. What if Noah sent someone after her, she thought. Nothing he'd do would surprise her at this point. Or maybe it was something even more horrible, something else that waited in the dark to devour her. Because of those possibilities, she decided to walk the entire way home instead of stopping and waiting by herself for the taxi. CJ walked a little faster. The sun had not fully set, so there was still time for her to make it back before the sky went completely black. The shadows she saw on the ground in front of her eluded to there being something large behind her. Or maybe above her. She couldn't tell.

What she did know was that it felt like someone had put weight in her shoes and the faster she tried to walk the slower she'd actually go. Her tears flowed faster as did her heart beat. Even as the shadows pulled her, she couldn't help but think about everything that had transpired in her life over the last two years.

Her father, Langston, dying to protect her honor and virtue. Her grandmother, the only connection left to her mother, dying of cancer. Her relationship with her Aunt Kara, the closest thing to a mother she'd ever known, crumbling under the knowledge of what Kara's husband and Langston's best-friend did to her as a child. Jonathan's profession of love and her inability to accept it; a factor in the disintegration of their friendship. And now this. Losing herself and her dignity over a backwoods, missionary preacher with beautiful eyes and the ability to hold her will hostage. All of these things, along with the great fear of the shadows that seemed to envelope her as she chased the sunset, consumed CJ as she moved her pace from a casual stroll to a full-on power walk and, a few seconds later, to a brisk jog.

Faster and faster CJ moved, and faster and faster the shadows hunted her. She watched the ground in front of her to monitor the shadows movements. She noticed the more she pondered her life, the bigger the shadows grew until she could almost feel the hotness of its breath on her neck. Her own breath became labored. Dampness spread under her arms, and beneath and between her breasts. That's when fear spoke to her. It told her the reason why she was rejected by Noah, why she was always rejected, was because she was not good enough. It told her that her faith and her God was impotent. That she should give up on life entirely because her destiny was uncertain, at best. The shadows danced and whispered all around her. When she covered her ears with her hands, their whispers became screams.

CJ's tears returned.

Why didn't I listen to Ms. Layla? She warned me.

Although CJ was now in a full out marathon run, she felt like she was running in place. She cried aloud at the parallels between what she was feeling now and what she'd always felt. *Barely making progress.*

Her sobs grew louder. She shouted to the air.

"WHY DO I HAVE TO FIGHT SO HARD?"

And then she remembered. She recalled Layla had shared with her that night on the beach that there was a war going on over her. She'd only half-believed the old woman back then, but it made sense now. Finally, CJ heard it. For the first time in what seemed like a lifetime, she heard that still, small Voice again. The one that had been muted and buried under all of her pain and rebellion.

Give it to me.

185

She still wasn't beyond questioning God and in that moment, He didn't mind.

"Give WHAT to you, Lord?"

All of it.

She knew what He meant. A full and uncompromised surrender of the hurt, the pain and the unforgiveness. He wanted it all.

This would not be easy. Rejection and loneliness had been with CJ since her birth and had created in her a sense of unworthiness she could never explain. Later, fear found an opening to oppress her soul when she was violated as a teenager. These were the shadows that chased her. These were the voices that distorted the Voice of the One she desired to hear the most. Out of breath, CJ continued to run as she screamed her surrender.

"I will! Take it Lord!"

As CJ ran, she prayed for the first time since she'd stood in the hospital waiting room anxiously awaiting news from the doctors about her father's injury. She prayed for forgiveness. She realized right then and there that all of her attitude and her acting out just caused her to hurt herself and the One who really could take it away. The One who also sought her and fought for her. She realized what she was seeking in Noah was what she should have been seeking in God. Peace. Unconditional love. A filling of the void left vacant by so much loss. Loss that she'd known since the day she was born.

As she prayed for God to take all of her pain, the burden that seemed to hold her grew lighter. The screaming, however, became louder.

CJ ran harder as the shadows seemed to get larger and larger with every word of prayer. But she couldn't stop. Praying, that is. She felt like she was shedding skin and breaking loose from all that pulled at her. There was something, maybe angels, fighting on her behalf and she loved the feeling. It felt like with every stride she was releasing some things and receiving others. Her heart, which just moments before had been crushed, was now being filled again. Each strenuous step became a symbol of God's ability to put her back together again. But then she heard the voice again. This time it commanded her.

Look behind you!

CJ didn't want to stop. She didn't want to face her demons. She was about 50 yards from the guesthouse, but in her mind she wanted to run forever towards the God she'd always known even if, for a season, she'd forgotten Him.

Look behind you now!

But CJ also didn't want to be disobedient. Certainly not now.

She slowed down. Panting heavily, she turned her head to look over her shoulder slightly and the final vestige of fear loosened its grasp.

Nothing.

There was nothing there. No animals. No red-brown brothers sent by a manipulative minister to kill her. Not even any shadows. CJ stopped running completely and bent over to catch her breath. She noticed the ominous feeling she'd sensed before was gone. The force that felt like it would devour her had vanished completely. Standing at the end of the trail within sight of the guesthouse, CJ fell to her knees and laughed. Joy overtook her as she realized whatever evil had chased her was gone forever. Left behind, it was just her and God.

I am here. I have always been here.

***

Layla was sitting on the couch reading her Bible when CJ came into the guesthouse still out of breath but smiling. The older woman stood up quickly and ran over to hug her. In another time, CJ would have stood rigid and unyielding to such a display of love, but this time she stepped fully into Layla's embrace. She felt like a child, but in a good way.

"I prayed, Ms. Layla!"

"Oh, honey. You did more than pray. Let me show you something."

187

The two walked over to the sofa and sat down. Layla opened her Bible to the place where she had marked and gave it to CJ.

"I was praying for you for the last hour and God led me to this scripture. Read what I have highlighted."

CJ read Deuteronomy 30:19. "Today, I have given you the choice between life and death, between blessings and curses. Now I call on heaven and earth to witness the choice you make. Oh, that you would choose life, so that you and your descendents might live!"

Layla said, "What did you pray for?"

CJ looked at Layla. "I prayed that God would take my pain."

"And He has," Layla replied.

CJ looked down at her dirty, loose red dress and was reminded of all she'd done.

"I asked Him to forgive me."

"And He did," Layla responded again.

"And…"

"And?"

"I asked him to forgive everyone who has hurt me."

Layla clapped her hands. "Thank you, Jesus!"

"That's the hard one, Ms. Layla. I did ask Him. But it's hard to really feel it, you know. I don't know how that is going to work in the natural," CJ said.

"Of course it is, sweetie. Don't you pay no attention to your feelings. They are about as deceptive as they come. You just pray God allows your feelings to catch up with what you desire in your heart. That's how you stay free in that area."

"Yes, m'am."

Suddenly, CJ's body started to ache with exhaustion. Layla noticed the heaviness in the young woman's eyes.

"You need to rest, babygirl. A good fight always takes the wind out of you." She winked at CJ who smiled authentically for the first time in a long while.

***

A week later, CJ packed her bags and prepared for her trip back home to Chicago. She truly felt free. Everything outside of her was the same. She'd still lost her mother and father. She'd still lost her grandmother. She'd still been the victim of abuse. But it was different now. The heaviness was gone. It reminded her of a song her Nana used to sing as she cleaned the house.

I was sinking deep in sin, far from the peaceful shore,
Very deeply stained within, sinking to rise no more,
But the Master of the sea, heard my despairing cry,
From the waters lifted me, now safe am I.

Love lifted me!
Love lifted me!
When nothing else could help
Love lifted me!

She smiled at the memory of her grandmother and then just as quickly, her thoughts turned to Ms. Layla. Her last week in Brazil had been a beautiful seven days spent writing, eating wonderful food and reading her Word with her friend. CJ had finally recognized how full of wisdom she was and, admittedly, tried to squeeze every bit of it out of her before she left. Layla didn't mind, though. She knew her assignment was coming to a close as well.

CJ walked into the living area with her bags. Layla sat in her favorite spot in the kitchen.

"You know, you never asked me what happened with Noah," CJ said.

Layla smiled. "It didn't matter. It was never about him anyway."

CJ knew the woman was right, but she still wanted to share the story. She needed to release it. Layla listened as CJ recounted the entire ordeal. She shook her head and then answered. "Well, honey, people will show you who they really are. No matter how much you may try to sugarcoat their

189

personalities or rationalize their behavior, the essence of a person can't be changed by another person. You can pray for them, but God does the changing."

"You're right. There were things I ignored. Things I saw but considered to be meaningless. Turned out those things meant a lot."

Layla nodded.

"But you know, Crystal. That same thing applies to those who love us, too."

CJ knew Layla had a gift and this time didn't question her.

"I hear God saying there is someone who He sent to you long ago, who has always loved you from a very pure place. He's not a perfect man. But he's always shown you who he was."

"And I ignored that also, huh?"

Layla was quiet. CJ got the message.

Changing the subject, Layla said, "So how are you feeling, in general, baby?"

"Clarity is a God send."

They both laughed.

"Yes it is, sugar. Yes. It. Is."

Layla walked over to CJ after she placed her own bags by the door.

"You know you broke something bigger than you last night, right?"

"Yeah, I guess I did."

Layla shook her head rapidly, "Don't guess, honey. Know it."

CJ beamed.

"God's going to use you now. You just watch and see."

CJ opened the door and signaled to the driver to help her with her bags. Since Pedro had left the day before, she had the first flight back to the states that morning.

With eyes filled with gratitude, she looked back at the old woman once more.

"I'm watching, Ms. Layla. Believe me, I'm watching."

Part Three:
Beginnings and Endings

The Concession

This wasn't the first time this had happened. It wasn't the first time victory was so close and yet Natas and his army of the most wretched demons succumbed to a swift and horrific defeat. It was beginning to feel inevitable. He'd done everything he possibly could do. Stripped the child of everything and everyone she loved. Whispered evil thoughts into her mind. Held her hostage to her past. Twisted her emotions so she remained confused about the true nature of love. Isolated her and sent her to the brink of sanity. He'd switched up his approach on every front and in the end, he still lost. What was the use of having a perfect strategy if it falters in the face of an even more perfect Enemy?

Natas didn't understand why the general always had him and the others fighting what seemed like a losing war. Or, how he kept them hopeful in spite of what seemed like inevitable defeat. Succeeding in a battle here and there, but never triumphing in the end. Was the general afraid to admit he was powerless? That his hands were tied? That he'd only be allowed to go so far in his efforts to win over the allegiance of these created beings.

This was especially true with the women in this family. Vivian Grace. Sasha Renee. Crystal Justine. It was like they had something special that the Enemy desperately wanted to use in the earth. After three generations of throwing trials and tribulations, attacks and accusations their way, it looked like they were finally going to accomplish it. Natas had exhausted his tactics. It was time to gather his troops, regroup and move on.

Complaining about it wouldn't change anything. This was his destiny to live out until the end of this age. Until the final confrontation with the Enemy. In the meantime, he would simply advance to the next assignment; targeting for evil the next man, woman, boy or girl in this generation or the next.

Chapter 21

Who is the real Crystal Justine Germaine? There were so many days I had no idea. No clue. She was hidden under layer upon layer of prepared statements, counterfeits, pseudo-happiness and an internal mess of thoughts that stayed in a constant state of disarray. To tell you the truth, I had no idea if the woman I was projecting to others was actually the woman I was meant to be. I only knew I'd worn a mask for so long it seemed like it was permanently adhered to my face. I was hungry for love. Hungry for acceptance. Hungry for someone, anyone, to heal me. It was as if somewhere along the way the real CJ, the one God designed for greatness, and the CJ I'd become comfortable with showing the world, had merged into one awfully needy woman. A woman who'd been handicapped by the pain and loss in her life and dwelled in a place of self-doubt. Although, I claimed otherwise, the only faith I had was in my circumstances.

On my flight home to Chicago, I had a revelation. Another one. Only this time it was a result of having 12 hours to finally read all of those letters that were sent to me in Brazil. Letters that, had I read them earlier, might have changed things a little bit.

Aunt Kara wrote me three letters. Each one helped me to shed the condemnation that tried to attach itself to my soul. In one, she said, *"You have always been like a daughter to me and I could never let anyone come in between us."* She asked me to forgive her for not reconciling with me sooner and she silenced any concerns I had about Benson. He'd moved somewhere down south with the young girl who was pregnant with his child. After reading her letters, I felt so much of a release I think I must have cried for an hour.

I'll be honest with you. My deliverance has not been without consequence. Jonathan's letters were even more difficult to read especially knowing he had moved on to another relationship. Ms. Layla's words resonated in my mind as I read his passion-filled words.

I don't know where I'd be without you in my life.

Growing up together, it was your face I saw when I thought about being married and having children. It is still your face I see.

I've loved you for what seems like forever and I'm frustrated that now I'm able to give you that love freely, you cannot, will not, receive it.

My sweet Jonathan. He taught me something through those letters. He taught me there is no point in loving someone if you can't love them in their imperfections. You don't love someone so they can change. People change because you love them. The kind of love Jonathan showed me throughout our friendship said real love covers you through your failures and wipes your unseen tears in the middle of the night. And maybe the greatest sacrifice of all. Loving them when they have walked away from you; the way I did him. And now I must return that love. I have to love him even as he loves someone else with all of the energy I now wish was directed toward me. But hey, why not? Isn't that what Jesus did? Didn't He look down and see us put others before Him, watch us fail and fall because we chose to love things and people that offered no where near the level of comfort and peace He could. And yet, He loves us anyway. So how much more should we, in wise and encouraging ways, love someone else intensely and passionately who may choose someone else. For that love lesson, I am forever thankful to Jonathan.

Am I sad? I am. After reading his letters, it was apparent I'd not only missed God during most of my time in

194

Brazil, but I missed out on the love and support of my best friend and the man I finally admit I've always loved. That is truly the hardest pill to swallow.

***

The bookstore manager tapped the microphone gently.

"Ladies and Gentlemen, I'd like to introduce to some and present to others our featured author for the evening, CJ Germaine."

In complete awe of where I was, I stood still for a moment taking it all in. So many people that loved me were here to cheer me on. My Aunt Kara and Aunt Toni. My godmother, Cassie. And yes, I believe even my mother, father and grandmother were watching me from above.

I wish I could have found Ms. Layla. I'd tried to look her up in order to invite her to my book release and signing, but I couldn't find her information anywhere. The Calypso Foundation even said they had no record of anyone by that name. I can't say that I'm surprised. Whether she existed in the natural or in the spiritual realm, I do know she was my angel, sent by God to protect me. To teach me. Isn't there a scripture that says we entertain angels unaware? How true that is.

Anyway, as I stood and looked out onto the audience, I couldn't help but think how much it took for me to get to this place. A place where I could share my story and possibly help some other young girl who, like I once did, feels empty and disconnected. My memoir is more than a book. It is my testimony.

I cleared my throat and spoke to the waiting crowd of family, friends and readers.

"People read the things I write and look at the places I've been and they say, 'wow, it must have taken a lot of courage to go through what you've been through and gone to the places you've gone.' And maybe for someone else, that would be absolutely true. Only for me, I spent most of my life running. Running away from who I was instead of trusting God to guide and heal me. As I think about it now, it probably would have been more courageous for me to stay in Chicago and confront the painful memories that tried to take me out of here and to develop the person God had destined me to become. But I didn't. Like the Israelites leaving the bondage of Egypt for the Promise Land and traveling forty years for what would have ordinarily been an eleven-day trip, I, too, took the long route to my promise. But I'm grateful for God's grace and mercy. Because in the end, here I stand. Blessed and favored beyond measure."

**

After I finished speaking, I read an excerpt from my book and then signed more copies. When the signing was over, I began packing my things when my Aunt Kara came over to my table.

"I'm so proud of you."

My heart filled as she kissed me on the cheek. I hugged her. "Thanks, Kara."

She picked up the purple and gold Kente tablecloth and began folding it up. I started putting away bookmarks and posters.

"Someone else is proud of you, too," she said with a look of amusement dancing in her eyes.

I looked up at her.

"Who?"

She pointed behind me and my heart stopped as I turned around quickly. It was Jonathan. I had no idea he was here.

Kara took my bag from my hands, still grinning.

"Go ahead and talk to him. I'll put the rest of these things away."

Can you imagine how nervous I was? My hands were shaking. He looked as good as ever. The closer he came the more the familiar scent of jasmine and musk assaulted my senses. I'd heard a rumor that he and Jordyn were planning to elope in Atlantic City, so when he finally stood in front of me, I couldn't help but to look at the ring finger on his hand.

It was empty and I was busted. He noticed me looking at his hand and raised it up to my face so I could get a closer look. He shook his head. Without saying a word, Jonathan took my hand and walked me over to the bookstore's café where we sat down and stared at each other for what seemed to me like a long time, but most likely was just a few minutes.

"You were wonderful."

I blushed under the admiring eyes of my long, lost friend.

"Thank you."

"You know, I discovered you right," he said jokingly.

I laughed.

"No, but seriously, Cris. I always knew you'd be something great."

It was great to hear him say that and in another time in my life, I would have basked in his approval out of need. But I had bigger fish to fry and I didn't want to waste anymore time with pleasantries.

"And I've always loved you," I said quickly.

I could tell he was surprised. His eyes were as wide as saucers. As scared as I was of rejection, I wasn't going to let that familiar spirit of fear stop me from saying what I should have said so long ago.

"I read your letters."

One of his eyebrows raised in response.

"I didn't read them until I got on the plane back to Chicago. Jonnie, I had to go through some stuff. I do know that. I had to be broken and I had to learn to love myself and God first. But sometimes in our going through, in being consumed by our own problems, we can miss God. I don't want to miss him again. Not when it comes to you."

The air was tense around us. Even though I knew that, whatever the outcome, I would be okay, I couldn't help but to be a little anxious about his reaction. I mean, I'd hurt him, too. It wasn't until I saw his eyes water and he responded that I knew everything was going to be as God had planned it.

"Do you want to know what I've been thinking, CJ?"

"No."

Jonathan smiled at my honesty.

"Well, too bad. I'm going to tell you. I've been thinking about that time when we were twelve and you told me you loved me."

I pretended to be shocked.

"I did not!"

Okay, I knew I did say that, but after the teasing he gave me when we were younger, I'm not trying to remember it. Not NOW.

Jonathan continued. "I've been thinking about all the moments we laughed at some corny inside joke we had."

I started laughing recalling some of the silly things we used to do. "Like when we'd see someone dressed really fly on the street and yell 'my friend first.'"

Jonathan chuckled at the memory.

"Yes, just like that."

Anxiety was now getting the best of me.

"Okay, so where are you going with this," I said.

I think I knew where he was going, but I wasn't going to pretend like I had a map. Hey, God is still working on me in the pride department.

"Let me be more clear. I've also been thinking about how we held each other through death and defeat, through devastation and despair."

Tears overflowed my eyes. His words were pulling down the final bricks in the wall I'd created to block out real love. I couldn't stop the emotions that were overwhelming me as my heart seemed to swell two times its size.

"I've been thinking that maybe its time you, no we, stop running from what's always been true between us."

When he used the word *running*, I knew it was God. And I knew I would never let this beautiful man go again.

Jonathan reached over and held my hand. I felt like I was six again. It was a new beginning.

***

Fear, Shame, Guilt and Unforgiveness all have pressed their evil presence into the hunger of my heart for long enough. I held onto them like a lottery ticket, not knowing it would only be the surrendering of the ticket that would get me my reward. I'm over its temptation, though. The joy my future holds and the peace that exists on the other side of

198

turmoil is a far better reward than the desperate attempts made by the enemy to make me forget the faith that has brought me this far. I can't be scared. I won't be scared. I have a purpose. A purpose that will step beyond this ridiculous fear of succeeding that I have. A purpose that will push past the hesitations and frustrations of the residual pains of my past. I am finally ready to explode into the most magnificent part of life.

You see, I'm what they call an *interruption*. I carry the same genes as my mother. I hold the same blood type as my grandmother. But while the blood that flows through my veins may be the same as those who have gone before me, I refuse to any longer carry the same baggage. I've chosen not to do so. It's critical I pass this new mind, if you will, along to my children in the future. It's critical I know who I am and Whose I am without a shadow of doubt. In all my flaws and in all those insecurities I nurtured, I no longer seek the love of other people, but I do desire that people see God's love in me. That unconditional love I ran from for so long.

Yes, I like how that sounds. I am an interruption in my bloodline. The final generation that puts an end to the madness and pursues destiny relentlessly. Through the fire and the trials and by the grace of God, I have put a stop to the attack on my family by changing the way I think and allowing the Spirit of God to flow freely in and through me.

Oh, one more thing. To every demon in hell who has pursued me, my mother, my grandmother and all of the women before us, you should have took me out when you had the chance because from this day forward, I am...we are...free.

Find out where it all began!

The Prequel

The Gospel According to Vivian Grace

Coming Soon
(I promise.)

Other Books by Tracey Michae'l Lewis

Divine Nepotism (poetry)

Write the Vision: A Collection of Essays

No Greater Love: A Poetry Collection

The Gospel According to Sasha Renee

CONTACT THE AUTHOR

Tracey Michae'l Lewis
c/o NewSEASON Books
PO Box 52545
Philadelphia, PA 19115
newseasonbooks@gmail.com